"WHERE THE DEVIL HAVE YOU BEEN?" MAX DEMANDED.

"Running," Buffy answered innocently.

"And you didn't care how I might worry about you? Couldn't you have at least left a note or given someone a message as to your whereabouts?"

"I don't have to answer to you or anybody, Max. I've been taking care of myself for years."

"Let's get something straight, shall we? As long as we're here, you answer to me. I have no intentions of going through any more hell getting you out of trouble. Don't ever go out alone again without telling me. That's an order."

"Don't bully me, Max," she warned. "I don't need all this chauvinistic domination. I don't need it and I don't want it."

CANDLELIGHT ECSTASY CLASSIC ROMANCES

CANDLELIGHT ECSTASY ROMANCES®

QUANTITY SALES

Most Dell Books are available at special quantity discounts when purchased in bulk by corporations, organizations, and special-interest groups. Custom imprinting or excerpting can also be done to fit special needs. For details write: Dell Publishing Co., Inc., 666 Fifth Avenue, New York, NY 10103. Attn.: Special Sales Dept.

INDIVIDUAL SALES

Are there any Dell Books you want but cannot find in your local stores? If so, you can order them directly from us. You can get any Dell book in print. Simply include the book's title, author, and ISBN number, if you have it, along with a check or money order (no cash can be accepted) for the full retail price plus $1.50 to cover shipping and handling. Mail to: Dell Readers Service, P.O. Box 5057, Des Plaines, IL 60017.

GENTLEMAN IN PARADISE

Harper McBride

A CANDLELIGHT ECSTASY CLASSIC ROMANCE

Published by
Dell Publishing Co., Inc.
1 Dag Hammarskjold Plaza
New York, New York 10017

ISBN: 0-440-12186-8

Printed in the United States of America

One Previous Edition

September 1987

10 9 8 7 6 5 4 3 2 1

WFH

To Our Readers:

As of September 1987, Candlelight Romances will cease publication of Candlelight Ecstasies and Supremes. The editors of Candlelight would like to thank our readers for 20 years of loyalty and support. Providing quality romances has been a wonderful experience for us and one we will cherish. Again, from everyone at Candlelight, thank you!

Sincerely,

The Editors

CHAPTER 1

Buffy ran to the net exultantly and grabbed her opponent's hand. The girl across the net grabbed her in a close, slippery hug, gasping, "Fabulous game, Buffy. You're just too good."

"Thanks, Cindy. I was lucky." They walked off the court together, one on each side of the net.

Buffy's legs and arms ached terribly, but she smiled triumphantly as a crowd of her tennis buddies surrounded her and a reporter with a tape recorder and microphone began a courtside interview.

"Congratulations, Miss Vallentine. Would you mind answering a few questions for the press?"

"Not a bit." Buffy grinned, raking perspiration from her brow. She had seen this brash, fast-talking reporter before. He was on the staff of the *Miami Times*.

"How does it feel to have won the Bahamas Invitational?" he quizzed.

"Great! It's been a marvelous tournament. The facilities here are superb. The people of Palm Isle Resort have put on a first-class affair here, and I am deeply indebted to Mr. Shepherd, the owner, for inviting me."

The reporter smiled broadly, and Buffy braced herself for more of his questions, which usually came fast and furiously. "It looked pretty rough for the both of you out there for a while. That last set was grueling, wasn't it?"

"Very." Buffy laughed. "Cindy and I have played each other before. I knew she would be a stiff opponent."

"It was a good game." The reporter nodded and cleverly tacked off in a different direction. "What are your immediate plans for the future? Is the rumor that you and Jeffrey Dunstan are getting married soon really true?" He grinned.

Buffy merely smiled coyly and whispered, "That's for me to know and for you to find out."

"Oh, come on!" he coaxed, his voracious appetite for news really whetted now. "Can't you tell us more than that?"

Buffy winked and wrinkled her cute retroussé nose teasingly as she leaned toward him. "It's none of your business." She tapped his chest gently with her racket before laughing and bouncing off the court, twirling her racket over her shoulder like a parasol.

She was on top of the world. She had beaten Cindy Croft by sheer grit today, for Cindy was a player with a great natural talent. But when it came to guts and endurance, Buffy had it over them all. She had been brought up in an orphanage, learning at an early age that courage was the stuff of life. When the manager of the orphanage, Mr. Johnson, a tennis enthusiast himself, had encouraged her to take up the sport, she threw herself into it with passionate intensity.

"Work hard," he had urged her daily after slamming it out with her on the courts. "You can already beat me. You might really go places with this thing."

"But I am so short," she had wailed, looking up at him from her diminutive five-foot-two-inch height. "Tennis players have long arms and long legs, don't they?"

He had looked down at her forever-blond and forever-curly head and smiled encouragingly. "You're strong, aren't you? You have determination, don't you? Your quickness and agility will see you through. Work. Show the world what you are made of."

That was ten years ago. Mr. Johnson had taken her to her first tournaments, where she seemed not to know the meaning of the word defeat. When she won the Florida Junior Women's title at the age of seventeen, she met Jeffrey, who had won the men's division. His wonderful family practically adopted her.

Mr. Dunstan offered her a job coaching tennis at his Miami country club. So after graduating high school, she left Mr. Johnson and the orphanage in Lakeland, Florida, to take up residence in a beautiful apartment overlooking the ninth fairway of the Waterbrook golf course.

For two years now she had been on her own. Many times she went to tournaments alone, but more often she went with Jeffrey and his parents. It seemed only natural that she and Jeffrey should become engaged. They had a great deal in common—their passion for tennis.

As tired as she felt, the nimble, petite young woman fairly bounded up the wide marble steps to the stately portico of Palm Isle Resort. Her blond, short, very curly hair clung damply to her forehead and neck, but her very chic red tennis dress still looked amazingly fresh.

At the top step she bent down to retie the shoelaces of one of her red tennis shoes. She was known for her fashionable tennis attire. Today's outfit was a bright cherry red except for fine white piping around the sleeves and neck. As she stooped her cherry-red tights peeped out provocatively from under the short skirt, showing the outline of a taut, boyishly slim derriere.

"May I congratulate you on your win," came a deeply masculine voice from behind her.

She straightened quickly and whirled around to face a tall, dark-haired man with the most piercing gray eyes she had ever seen.

For a moment that seemed like an eternity she allowed herself to be captured by them. "Thank you," she said, smiling as she tore away and rushed into the wide main entrance.

When she reached her room she fumbled with her door key, seeing nothing before her but a tall man with thick dark hair and friendly, but somehow penetrating, gray eyes. Finally the lock clicked and the door to her spacious room swung open.

She immediately saw a large spray of red roses with a ribbon of congratulations from the management. Fast work. The hotel seemed to be on top of everything.

9

She scuffed off her tennis shoes, stuffed them into a plastic bag along with her tennis dress, crammed the bag into her already packed suitcase, then padded off to the shower.

In less than an hour she was dressed in a well-fitting baby-blue pantsuit. She combed her hair in careless curls around her head and sat down to a lighted mirror to do her makeup.

There was a knock at the door and Cindy's voice: "Buffy, may I come in?"

She went reluctantly to unlock the door, stepping back silently to admit her friend.

"Buffy, Mom and Dad wanted me to ask you to come to the banquet with us tonight. Mom is up in the air about your being here all alone."

Cindy, still dressed in her pink tennis dress, plopped down on a velvet settee and fiddled with her long brown hair. "I tell you, it's maddening to be eighteen and still tied to the proverbial apron strings. They won't let me out of their sight. I keep telling Mom how you were going it alone at my age. She just looks up to heaven and clicks her tongue."

She made a face aping her mother and mimicked in a falsetto voice, " 'That's Buffy! It's dangerous the way she gallivants all over the country on her own. Why, it's a wonder she hasn't been murdered, or worse!' "

Buffy burst into laughter. "What could be worse?"

Cindy pursed her lips and gave her friend a teasing look. "If you had a mother, you would know. I've been warned since the onset of puberty to look out for the ravening wolves out there. Don't let them get near. One little kiss sparks off an explosion of mad passion that cannot be assuaged until you are totally ravished." She sighed as if she longed for that fate.

Buffy gave a tinkling little giggle and smiled. "Your mother is sweet."

"My mother is a Victorian prude," Cindy said sourly. "At this rate I'll never get a boyfriend."

Buffy put down the lipstick she had been about to use

10

and became very serious. "There were times in my life, Cindy, that I would have given anything to have had a mother—even if she were a Victorian prude."

"Oh, I know, Buffy. I'm sorry I sounded like a brat. It must have been pretty tough growing up in an orphanage. I know I'm fortunate." She stood up to leave. "I've got to go and shower now. We'll come by for you at six-thirty."

"No, Cindy, I won't be at the banquet tonight. I'm leaving on the next flight out."

"What are you talking about!" Her friend stopped in frozen amazement. "You're the guest of honor."

"I just can't make it. I had no idea when I accepted the invitation that there would be a banquet the night of the finals. I just assumed the trophies and prize money would be given directly after the match."

"Didn't you read your brochure?" Cindy sounded exasperated. "The big finale is a banquet, trophies, and speeches, and a fantastic show afterward featuring different styles of island dancing."

"I didn't know until yesterday," Buffy explained. "McMutt got my brochure and ate the last page before I could read it." She sat before the mirror despondently.

"Oh, that stupid dog. Why you keep that Heinz-57-Variety mutt, I'll never know."

"She is silly," Buffy admitted ruefully. "But I love her anyway. By the time I found out about the banquet, Mrs. Dunstan had already made all the arrangements for the wedding."

"Wedding! For heaven's sake! You're marrying Jeffrey tonight and you're here winning a tennis tournament, instead of in Miami, where you belong on your wedding day?"

"I have time to get back," Buffy answered defensively. "I couldn't let this tournament go by just because I'm getting married." She looked at her watch. "I've got to split now to catch my flight. Please explain things for me, Cindy. You can tell them all at the banquet tonight. By then it will be too late for the press to crash our wedding ceremony. Tell Mr. Shepherd I'm sorry." She grabbed her purse in one hand and her suitcase in the other. "Tell them to send my money to me at their convenience."

She sailed out the door, Cindy following close behind. "I'll write the hotel a letter of apology. Frankly, I thought you would win the final match anyway, and no one would notice if I didn't show up." She clamored into the elevator and smiled at her astonished friend as the doors closed between them.

It was true that she had expected Cindy to win. Cindy had more natural ability. She was longer of limb. But she had not been aggressive enough. That had been her undoing. Buffy had played like an atomic fireball consistently throughout the match, which had worn her friend out.

Of course, she felt like a rat not showing up for that nice Mr. Shepherd's wonderful banquet. He was a very proper and courteous British gentleman with mild and fatherly dove-gray eyes.

He'll think I'm rude, but I just can't help it, she cried to herself. I must catch my plane in twenty minutes. There's no time to explain things to him myself. I couldn't mention it before, for fear it might have leaked to the press. Then Jeffrey would have blown his stack; he hates publicity on his personal life. She actually felt rattled and not at all up to getting married.

The elevator doors rolled open upon reaching the ground floor, and she rushed over to the desk to check out. She looked up briefly as she dropped her suitcase and slid the key across the counter with a grating ring.

"Is someone chasing you, Miss Vallentine?" asked the same man she had seen on the portico. He caught her key before it dropped off the edge of the desk, and flashed her a questioning look.

"I have to catch a plane in twenty—no, fifteen minutes," she explained, quickly looking at her wristwatch.

"I see," he said coolly. And she watched in amazement as his eyes turned to steel. "Running out on us, then?"

"I must. I have to get back before tonight." She had never seen him at the desk before and wondered if he was new on the job. "Do you know Mr. Shepherd, by any chance?"

"I'm acquainted with him, yes," he answered in clipped tones. It was apparent that this man also was from England, for he spoke the same precise, well-modulated English as did Mr. Shepherd.

"Oh, please tell him," said Buffy as she picked up her suitcase, "that I . . . that, well . . ." The man's eyes were now the color of hard charcoal. ". . . Thanks for the hospitality," she finished feebly.

She turned then and fled through the front doors to hail a taxi, several of which were always parked outside in the large circular driveway.

The driver made good time and she tipped him handsomely as she rushed into the airport terminal and made her way over to the line of people in front of the Eastern desk. While she waited her turn she listened for the arrival of her flight.

She was quite puzzled by the time it was her turn to speak to the fine-featured ebony native at the desk. "Has flight three-oh-five arrived yet?" she asked. "I haven't heard it called. Have I missed it?"

"I'm sorry, miss," said the native politely. "Eastern went on strike this morning. There will be no flights coming in today at all. And perhaps not tomorrow."

"B-but," Buffy spluttered, "I must get to Miami."

"I'm sorry," reiterated the woman. And it seemed to Buffy that she wasn't the least bit sorry.

"Look. I'm getting married tonight," explained Buffy. "I have to get back. It's all arranged. They're just waiting on me—the bride." Her voice rose to a hysterical pitch.

The woman shrugged her uniformed shoulders and went about shuffling papers on her desk. Buffy wondered how many times that day she had listened to similar emergency situations.

"Next, please." She looked up, dismissing Buffy with a glance.

"Just a minute!" Buffy exploded. "What about a flight on another airline? What about Florida Air? Are they going out this afternoon?"

"The last Florida Air of the afternoon just left, miss. The next one leaves at seven o'clock this evening."

"But that's too late," she wailed, knowing she was making a scene. Seven o'clock was the time set for the wedding. That was when the organ would ring out with the "Wedding March" and all eyes would be on the bride. But there would be no bride.

"Perhaps you can find someone with a private plane to take you out, miss. I'm sorry. Next, please."

Buffy moved away from the desk in a huddle of confusion. Jeffrey would be livid if she called him and told him she wouldn't be able to make their wedding. He had asked her not to come to this tournament. He had said that it was cutting the time too closely.

To make matters worse a driving afternoon thunderstorm was coming down in bucketfuls. And she was deathly afraid of storms. It was a phobia of hers that had survived childhood. Nevertheless, she squared her shoulders and bravely ran out into it, wading through a gigantic mud puddle to get to a taxi. The driver didn't get out to help her with her suitcase, so she heaved it into the backseat and growled angrily while getting in herself, "To Palm Isle. And step on it."

While riding back to the resort she searched her mind frantically for a solution to her dilemma. Perhaps Mr. Shepherd would know someone she could hire to fly her to Miami. He was her only hope.

She stepped out of the taxi and the rain stopped as suddenly as it had started, the sun coming out in a blindingly yellow display that made her feel like a fugitive from a shipwreck.

The driver was all smiles now, white teeth gleaming in a smoothly black face. She took her bag from him roughly and muttered a scathing, "Thanks."

Her expensive leather heels squelched out little puddles of water all the way across the lobby as she made her way to the desk. What little control she normally had over her temper was slipping fast.

A woman was at the desk now. She was intensely grate-

14

ful that the handsome gray-eyed man was no longer around to see her condition, for her suit was clinging wetly to her goose-pimply skin, and her hair hung in little amber corkscrews all around her head.

"May I help you?" the woman asked crisply, backing away from Buffy involuntarily as if she were a sewer rat.

"Where can I find Mr. Shepherd?" she inquired firmly.

"I don't think Mr. Shepherd is seeing anyone this afternoon." The clerk smiled at Buffy's folly.

"I don't give a damn what you think," she countered heatedly. She wasn't at all used to being put down, and this afternoon's turn of events had completely rocked her good manners. "Now, where the hell is he?"

"His suite is down the hall." She pointed. "First door to the right."

Buffy thanked her with as much dignity as she could muster, picked up her bag, and squished her way down the hall.

She rang his doorbell and waited impatiently, hoping she wasn't still dripping too badly. She had made up her mind she wouldn't go into his room, of course. She would merely apologize for her condition, explain the circumstances, and ask if he knew of anyone who could take her off the island.

She gasped as the door opened and she was stabbed by a pair of now familiar, piercing gray eyes, which quickly twinkled with amusement as they looked down at her.

"I-I'm sorry," she stuttered. "I've obviously come to the wrong door. I was looking for Mr. Shepherd."

"Then you've come to the right place, indeed. Please come in. I rather expected you couldn't get off today." The man was really too cool, and Buffy, in her state of wreckage, felt decidedly at a disadvantage.

"I couldn't come in. I'm all wet. I got caught in the storm," she explained feebly.

He smiled. And she wondered fervently who this unusually attractive man was. She looked straight ahead at the third button on his black silk shirt, trying not to notice the patch of dark masculine chest hair exposed above it.

15

"If you would just tell me where I can find Mr. Shepherd, please. I have urgent business to discuss with him." She shivered in the cold air conditioning as her wet clothes turned clammy and uncomfortable.

"Do come in," he ordered, pulling her into his room unceremoniously. "You're looking for my father, whose suite is the penthouse in the right wing. But for now you'll have to make do with me."

He reached for her suitcase and she released it automatically. He took it into his large, spacious bathroom and motioned her to follow.

"Change out of those wet things before you really become ill," he ordered. "Then we shall discuss your dilemma over a warming drink. I am really quite anxious to discover why the illustrious winner of our tennis tournament would leave in such a flap, only to come back even more hurriedly through a driving rain."

"I feel just terrible imposing on you like this, Mr. Shepherd. It's a lot of bother for you to take time to—"

He held up a restraining hand. "Off you go now. I've quite made up my mind about you."

She smiled up at him, wrinkling her nose mischievously. He really was sweet, and didn't seem to mind helping her at all. "You know, Mr. Shepherd, I like your accent."

He folded his arms across his broad black silk shirt and leaned against the doorjamb. "I find yours quite charming, too." His mouth tilted up at the corners.

"But I don't have an accent," she protested, raising her delicate brows in surprise.

"Oh, but indeed you have," he contradicted. "I believe you Americans call it a thick Southern drawl. Now get into dry things." He leaned forward and pulled the door closed, adding, "Immediately."

She looked around the spotless white-tiled bathroom. A huge round black tub was sunken into a raised platform, and she longed to turn the gold knobs and run it to the brim with warm water. But there was no time for a leisurely soak. Instead, she quickly undressed, took a large fluffy black towel from the linen closet, and rubbed herself

16

down vigorously. Then she stuffed her wet suit into the plastic bag that held her tennis clothes, hoping they wouldn't all be a moldy mess by the time she reached home.

Home. Would she get there on time? Dressing quickly in a chocolate-brown pantsuit trimmed with white dots, she bit her lips in frustration. If only this young Mr. Shepherd knew of someone with a private plane. She repaired her makeup and combed her now drying hair around her head in a wreath of golden curls.

She hadn't seen the junior Mr. Shepherd the first two days of the tournament. Perhaps he had been away on business. Snapping her suitcase shut, she wondered fleetingly how old he was. About thirty-three or -four, she imagined. Was he married? Decidedly not. He didn't have that lean and hungry look that marked the married man.

By the time she opened the door, she felt much better. She walked over to him and smiled congenially. She went barefoot, since her only pair of dress shoes were soaked clear through.

He was standing in front of glass sliding doors, making a silhouette that was broader and taller than she remembered him actually being, which was enough. The glare from the sun coming through the sheer draperies behind him made it impossible to read his face.

He lifted a tinkling drink and took a sip as he remarked, "There. Feeling better now?"

"Yes, thank you."

"I fixed you a drink." He handed it to her from a nearby bar. "Not knowing your preferences, I decided rum and coke would be safe."

She took the proffered drink, feeling somewhat like a misplaced dwarf, then escaped to the couch. The man really had to be well over six feet tall.

"I don't usually drink at all," she confessed. "My strict training doesn't permit it. But thank you." She sipped tentatively, and finding it to her liking, she tucked her bare feet comfortably under her in a flexible, childlike position.

"Now," he began, still bathed in the glare from the window. "Perhaps you will tell me why it is so necessary for you to leave Nassau. Didn't you like the roses I sent you?" he asked with an edge of sarcasm. "Perhaps yellow is your favorite."

"Were you responsible for ordering the flowers? They were gorgeous. Thank you very much."

"Then it wasn't the color of the posies, I take it, that set you against us so that you wanted to leave before the banquet. A banquet, I might add, at which you are the guest of honor."

"You don't understand," she said hurriedly. "I'm not offended at all. Your father, and everyone here at the resort, has been wonderfully kind and hospitable." She squinted at the dark shape in the white light of the window and sighed deeply. "It's a secret," she began, "but since I need help, I suppose I can tell you."

"Tell me what?" He raised his glass again.

"I'm getting married tonight."

He took a deep gulp of his drink and stood immobile for a moment. "I see. Who is the lucky fellow?"

"Jeffrey Dunstan. We're keeping it quiet because of the press."

"Jeffrey Dunstan, the tennis pro?" He moved over to the bar and set down his empty glass soundlessly.

"Yes. So you see, I must get back to the States immediately. Mr. Shepherd, do you know anybody, anybody at all, who can take me off this island?"

"Call me Max, please." He walked toward her with pantherlike agility and she wondered if he too was an athlete. His movements were too sure, his body too lean for it to be otherwise.

"I might be able to arrange it." He took a place beside her on the couch.

"Oh, marvelous," she breathed.

"But it doesn't take long to fly to Miami, so we have plenty of time. Please finish your drink and relax a bit. You've had a strenuous time of it, haven't you?" He smiled then and pierced her again with those unfathomable gray eyes.

18

She rested her head on the cushion, unknowingly brushing her blond curls against his hand, and sipped at her drink.

"So you're madly in love, Miss Vallentine."

"What?" Then realizing he was referring to herself and Jeffrey, she couldn't resist giggling.

"Then you're not madly in love, I take it. Yet you're getting married tonight. It's a puzzle."

She stared at him for a moment, taking in the deeply tanned regular features, the straight black brows, the faint cleft in his squarish chin. "Madly in love? What does that mean these days?" She waved airily. "It went out with fairy tales. Jeffrey and I are compatible, and we're comfortable together. That's what counts."

"Oh, really." His black brows shot up. "Such cynicism in one so young is rare indeed, Miss Vallentine. You're certainly not the usual starry-eyed bride. I gather your fiancé shares this rather sterile philosophy of marriage. But of course he must. No man looking forward to his wedding night would allow his bride to wear herself out on a tennis court hundreds of miles away."

Buffy nearly choked over her drink as her temper rose mercurially. "He understands my passion for tennis. I'm on my way to Wimbledon, you know." She tossed her curls confidently and struggled to keep a grip on her temper. Who did this man think he was, anyway, to question her motives for marrying Jeffrey, much less her condition on her wedding night?

"Look, are you going to make arrangements for me to fly out of here? If not, I'll go elsewhere for help." She got up to leave.

"Just a minute," he halted her. "One more question before I make the arrangements."

"What is it?" she asked irritably.

"Why did you accept our invitation in the first place, knowing you would not be able to attend the banquet. It doesn't seem quite fair to us."

She sighed and sat back down. "I'm really sorry about that. My mongrel, McMutt, is fond of eating my mail. She

19

took a particular liking to your glossy brochure. I-I simply didn't know about the banquet until after I arrived."

He grinned. "A mongrel? I would picture you with a smaller dog. A poodle perhaps." His eyes went to her closely cropped, springy curls.

"McMutt suits me fine. I rescued her from the Humane Society when she was a little furry puppy about to be put to sleep. We jog together everyday when I'm home. She's undisciplined, neurotic, and totally devoted to me." She looked impatiently at her watch.

As if on cue, he moved to the telephone, lifted the receiver, and dialed a number. "Hello. Frank? Max here. Have my plane ready for takeoff in twenty minutes. I know you haven't had time to go over it since my return from South Caicos, but it can't be helped. This is rather important." He looked at Buffy intently. "I'm sure everything is all right."

Buffy sat stunned for a moment after he replaced the receiver. "Y-you're going to take me?" she stammered.

"But of course. I can't have a girl as lovely as you miss her wedding, can I?"

"B-but I'm sure you haven't the time. You must be a very busy man. I couldn't put you out like this."

"Nonsense. My father has been urging me to take some time off. If you'll just wait a moment while I pack a few things. I might even stay on in Miami for a few days."

"You're sure it's not putting you out?"

"Positive." He smiled charmingly.

Her honey-brown eyes were warm with gratitude. "How can I ever thank you enough. I'll pay you."

"No need for that," he assured her gallantly. "Just consider it a gesture of chivalry."

"Rescuing the damsel in distress?" she teased. "I thought that went out of style long ago."

"Not at all," he assured her in his dry British accent. "No more than the mad, passionate love we mentioned earlier." He walked to his bedroom door and opened it, saying, "But I suppose you Americans look at things a bit differently." He closed the door behind him, leaving her dumbfounded.

Why, the man had more brass than a tack factory! What did he mean by that last crack? It was one thing to insult her but quite another to lambaste the whole American population. She fumed inwardly. For all his courteousness he was an overbearing oaf. Did he think all Americans, in general, incapable of deep feelings? Did he think her a fool for marrying Jeffrey even though it wasn't a storybook romance? Compatibility was a very good basis for marriage, she reasoned. After all, the divorce courts were full of the wreckage and carnage of marriages that had started out with a storm of passionate feeling.

When he came back into the living room he was dressed in white pants that precisely fitted firm, dented hips. His shirt was a soft-looking navy blue rolled up to the elbows and open at the neck to reveal a shiny gold chain that lay in a mat of thick chest hair at the base of his throat.

"Just one more call before we go." He smiled as he walked to the phone.

Oh, a man like Max would believe in passionate love for sure, Buffy thought. Why, one look into those compelling gray eyes and a woman would sink as if she had a lead weight tied to her foot. And as for marriage, why should he bother.

"Hello. Dad? I'm taking off to Miami for a day or two." He gave Buffy a soft, amiable look, then continued, "Our Miss Vallentine is going along. She won't be making it to the banquet tonight. Seems she has made previous arrangements to get married." He laughed. "No, not to me, unfortunately." Buffy's mouth twisted sarcastically. Big joke. "Yes, I will. Take care. Call you later."

He hung up and moved toward the luggage. "He told me to offer you his fondest felicitations. Are you ready to go?"

"Yes, please," she answered stiffly, trying not to warm to him.

"Don't worry," he assured her on the way to the airfield as she sat brittlely in his silver Corvette. "I'll have you at

21

your apartment by five-thirty. Plenty of time to get ready for the big affair. What are you wearing?" he asked conversationally, apparently knowing at least one subject that would send a woman talking nonstop for hours on end.

"I don't know. Mrs. Dunstan ordered my gown. It's to be in my apartment when I arrive."

"You didn't even select your own wedding dress?" he asked, amazed. "This whole situation gets muckier by the moment."

"I haven't had time to go shopping lately. I've been on tour for the past six weeks, just being able to get home for a day or two at a time. Since I'm a perfect size five, Mrs. Dunstan volunteered to take care of the dress matter. She has wonderful taste in clothing."

"I'm sure," he murmured.

"She keeps McMutt for me, too, while I'm away. I've really missed her lately. I hope Mrs. Dunstan hasn't spoiled her and made her too fat."

"So you've missed McMutt but not poor Jeffrey." He raised his dark brows, looking at her askance.

"I didn't say that," she protested.

"You didn't have to. You've barely mentioned his name. I find it difficult to believe you'll be sharing a wedding bed with him tonight. He doesn't even seem to have a place in your heart, with the capable Mrs. Dunstan, your lovable dog, and your all-consuming tennis career occupying so much of your affection."

"You're despicable," she hissed. "What gives you the right to criticize my personal life? I've only just met you."

He parked the car in a garage at the airfield and came around to open her door. She stood up and found herself in a wide prison made by his arms, for one hand still held the door while the other rested against the car. He bent his head down and looked at her keenly.

"Look. I'm not trying to needle you. But I am in this, whether you like it or not. I've become quite concerned over this whole travesty of a marriage arranged by the estimable Mrs. Dunstan."

She looked down at her still damp leather shoes, refusing to look at him directly. "You're making a mistake," he went on, "and deep down you know it."

All of a sudden she felt like an awkward and erring child. "I love Jeffrey. And he loves me." She ducked under his arm and walked out of the garage.

"You are grateful to him. That is not a solid enough basis for marriage," he argued, coming up behind her. "Oh, hello, Frank." He turned to a garage mechanic dressed in white greasy coveralls. "All set?"

"Yes, sir. But please realize that I haven't gone over her good since you got back." Frank's forehead puckered into a frown. "She should be okay, though. She's not even a year old." He was speaking of the plane as if it were a living thing. "But she's seen a lot of miles lately," he worried.

"These Cessnas are solidly built," Max assured the mechanic. "Don't look like such an old lady. I haven't crashed yet. And I've flown thousands of miles. Will you get the luggage for us?"

He grabbed Buffy's arm and led her to a bright yellow twin engine aircraft. "I wish I could talk you into staying at the resort for a few more days," he posed tentatively, "just to think over this thing."

"No way," she stated flatly. "I couldn't disappoint the Dunstans like that."

"I've a good mind not to take you, after all," he threatened, his eyes looking thunderous.

"You had better, after leading me all this way!" Buffy gasped.

"I shall," he said through clenched teeth. "But quite reluctantly."

"My knight in tarnished armor," she jibed. "What would I do without your brotherly concern and timely advice?"

He gripped her arm tighter. "What do your parents say about this comfortable, compatible marriage Mrs. Dunstan has arranged for you?"

"I have no parents. I am an orphan."

"No family at all?"

"None."

"God, what a mess!" He nearly carried her bodily up the portable steps and pushed her into the seat next to his. "Thanks, Frank," he said, waving as the amazed mechanic shut the door. He looked at Buffy briefly and coldly as he settled himself at the controls. "I've nearly lost my temper, you know."

Buffy, who had never been a champion at keeping a tight rein on hers, burst out angrily, "Who the hell do you think you are? I've known you only for a couple of hours, and you think you can meddle in my personal life."

"Someone has to," he said crisply, reaching over to fasten her seat belt.

"I'm twenty years old. I've been on my own for two years." Her usually warm, friendly eyes were now flashing angrily.

"You don't know your own mind. You're a child," he stated briefly, then started up the plane to drown out her angry protests.

CHAPTER 2

As the plane left the ground Buffy had a feeling of uneasiness. Max seemed comfortable enough at the controls, yet the plane seemed little more than a garishly painted tin can. It was unnerving to entrust oneself to such a flimsy piece of metal with only the blue sky above and the beautiful aquamarine water below.

"You're off New Providence Island now. We're heading west, for Miami," Max told her. "Below are some of the best fishing waters in the world for bass, lobster, shrimp, and the great sea turtle. The darker blue patches are deep holes of water where the great black jewfish lie."

"You can see the water much better in a small plane, can't you?" she remarked in a small, anxious voice. "I feel as if I could reach down and trail my fingers in it."

"It's farther away than it looks." He smiled. "Is this your first ride in a small plane?"

"Yes. And I think I prefer jets."

"You won't, once you get a taste of this. Flying is much more fun and exciting in small craft."

She closed her eyes and swallowed a lump of fear. "Fun, exciting," she choked. "If only I could be sure we weren't going to belly flop on that sapphire-blue sea. I'll bet it has all the elasticity of concrete when hit from this height."

"Don't worry," he chuckled, reaching over to pat her hand. "I know what I'm doing."

They soared along for a few silent minutes, and just as she was beginning to relax, he jerked her upright by remarking, "We seem to be having a spot of difficulty here. Nothing to worry about."

"What is it?" she asked, alarmed.

"One of the engines is cutting up. It will come right in a moment." He studied the controls grimly and seemed to be listening intently at the cuts and groans of one of the engines.

"Oh, lord. We're going to crash," Buffy groaned.

"Optimistic, aren't you? Instead of snivelling, perhaps you could look out on the left wing and tell me what you see."

She craned her neck and uttered a stifled shriek. "I-It's on f-fire!" she babbled, pointing out the window with a shaky finger.

"The wing?"

"No, th-the thingamabob that runs the propeller, th-the motor, I guess." She was fast becoming hysterical. All of the courage she possessed on the courts was nowhere to be found up in this vast expanse of air. "It's sparking and getting ready to blow up."

She clenched her fists over her eyes and struggled against panic. If she was going to die, she would die with dignity, for that was how she had tried to live.

He set the controls and looked out at it himself. Then he settled wordlessly back in his seat. After a few silent moments he commented, "I'm sorry about this. That engine does seem to be burning out fast."

"I'm not blaming you." She sighed tremulously, then suddenly blurted out, "Look, if I don't make it, and you do . . ."

He looked surprised and started to interrupt.

"No, let me say this," she rushed on. "If I die, please see about McMutt. The Dunstans will be sad for a while, but they don't need me. McMutt, however, will be lost if I never show up again." The tenseness of the situation caused her to grope for self-honesty. "And, if it matters at all, I admit that I might not be in love with Jeffrey." Large tears welled up in her drowned-pansy eyes. "You

26

see," she quavered, turning to his startled expression, "I don't even know what love is."

A broad, beautiful smile spread across his face. "My darling Buffy." He took her hand and held it tenderly. "I have no intentions of allowing us to crash."

"Promise?" she asked in a high, watery voice.

"Promise," he stated firmly. "Now you just relax and trust me." Then he turned her hand over and kissed the palm, sending a strange prickling sensation up her arm, which spread quickly to the vicinity of her heart and exploded there like warm fireworks.

During the next twenty minutes he was a dynamo of efficiency. He radioed someone named Myaka and explained that he was flying on one engine. The melodious voice of Myaka came through, urging him to land as soon as possible.

He banked the plane sharply to the right, and Buffy felt certain they would dip right into the turquoise-blue sea. She closed her eyes and didn't open them again until she felt the plane touch down with miraculous smoothness on dry, solid ground. They taxied to a stop on a deserted runway.

He turned to her and unsnapped her seat belt. "There. You're all in one piece. It wasn't nearly as bad as you thought. The deathbed confessions were not necessary, although I found them immensely interesting, to say the least. We were crippled, yes. But not incapacitated."

He opened the door and hopped out as a short black native ran over to the plane, grinning widely. "Hello, Mr. Shepherd. So nice you come here. We miss you when you stay away so long."

"Glad to see you again, Myaka." Max smiled as he handed the native their luggage, which he quickly deposited in a golf cart nearby.

Buffy, having regained full composure by now, appeared at the door of the plane and Max lifted her down with such a charmingly handsome smile that she felt she would melt into the runway like a spot of butter.

"This is my passenger, Miss Vallentine," he told Myaka.

"I was flying her to Miami when that engine cut out on us."

"Happy to meet you, miss." Myaka showed her two even rows of teeth, which flashed ridiculously white in his midnight-velvet face. "You both please go on up to house," he spoke in melodious pidgin English. "Loa make coffee and sandwiches. I stay here. Try to fix engine."

"Thanks, Myaka," Max said as he led Buffy to the white golf cart, which had a gay striped canopy with a multicolored fringe.

"There are no cars on this island?" Buffy asked interestedly.

"No need for them," Max explained. "The island is only one mile across at its widest part. There are no stores or restaurants or tourists traps, or anything. Only Ponsonby's Palace, as we call it, up on the rocks."

He steered the cart in the direction of the cliff, and they whizzed along silently in the little battery-operated vehicle as if by magic.

Buffy was enchanted by what she could see of the island. There were wide lakes of undulating grass that ran down sloping hills to a glistening white sandy beach. Black rugged rocks roughened the serene landscape, giving it character, and a dreamy breeze fanned her face and ruffled playfully in her curls. The highest part toward which they were moving was lush with greenery and wildly exotic flowering plants. The narrow road, paved thickly with pine needles, was guarded by many ancient Australian pines that seemed to whisper of peace and contentment.

"I never knew places like this existed," she said dreamily.

"Dad and I call it Ponsonby's Paradise. We vacation here frequently. Dad and Lord Ponsonby practically grew up together. They both sold their estates in England at about the same time. Ponsonby bought this island; Dad built Palm Isle Resort. Sometimes I think Ponsonby had the right idea all along. This place is a utopia. Dad, however, wanted to leave me with more than a title and a small island."

She swallowed this information with a loud gulp. "You are an English lord? An aristocrat? An English gentleman?"

"Forget it." He smiled. "Not the part about my being a gentleman, of course." He stopped the cart and handed her out of it as if she were royalty. "I do hope I'm that. But about the title—it is of no consequence in this part of the world. Actually, fancy titles tend to put people off. Make them uncomfortable, you know."

"Yes, I know," Buffy choked. She turned to face Ponsonby's Palace, which did not look at all like a palace but several sprawling modern houses set together at different angles. The structure was surrounded by small sloping hills either emerald with bright sod or flaming with tropical flowers.

Huge potted ming trees graced either side of intricately carved oaken double doors that opened immediately to reveal the welcoming face of a black woman. This was Loa, of course.

"Mr. Shepherd, sir. I am so happy to see you again. So sorry about your airplane," she sympathized in rich singsong English undertoned with a British accent. "But so glad you were made to land here." She beamed a smile on Buffy and captured her heart immediately, for it was a gentle smile, full of grace. "Come in, please. Refreshments are on the patio."

Max left their luggage in the foyer and led Buffy through a wrought iron gate into an immense sunken living room, which was completely glass enclosed on the sea side.

She walked to the windows, the scene taking her breath away. There was an enormous pool with a natural rock waterfall. Since the house was built on a rocky hill, the land beyond the pool area dropped away into blue air and even bluer sea.

"Come along, Buffy. You must be nearly starved. I know I am," Max said.

The sandwiches were delicious—generous amounts of creamy chicken salad and lettuce between slices of what appeared to be homemade bread. Tall frosty glasses of iced tea garnished with thin slices of lime were continually being replenished by Loa.

Once during the meal, Buffy roused out of her dreamy, relaxed euphoria long enough to ask, "When do I meet the owner of this fabulous place?"

"Ponsonby is on a European tour. I'm afraid he may not be back for several weeks."

"Do you think Myaka can fix the plane in time for us to get to Miami before seven?"

He stirred his coffee slowly. "Perhaps. Can you accept it if he cannot?"

"I'll have to, won't I." She got up and walked to the pool, kneeling to touch the water with her pink-nailed fingertips. Maybe it wasn't meant to be. Maybe it just wasn't ordained. She was a jumble of conflicting emotions. This morning, marrying Jeffrey had seemed so right. Now she wasn't sure of anything.

"How is the water?"

She smiled at him openly. "Cool. Nice."

At that moment Myaka walked up to Max and apologized. "Sorry, Mr. Shepherd, the engine is . . ." He made a poofing sound between his lips, indicating that the engine had gone up in smoke. "Plane not safe to fly. I call Nassau for part. It come on supply boat in maybe two weeks, maybe less."

"Two weeks!" Buffy breathed in disbelief. "Is there some other way to get off this island, Max?" she asked, turning her honey-brown eyes on him.

He took a sip of his coffee and set it down thoughtfully. "I can call Dad. He could get here . . . let's see . . ." He consulted his watch. "It's five now. He could get here in his plane by seven, perhaps."

"No!" She stated emphatically. "That's out of the question. I couldn't ask it of your father. I wouldn't! Besides, it would disrupt the whole banquet. He is the master of ceremonies. I'll just have to call Miami and tell Jeffrey to postpone the wedding." Somehow, by saying this, she was immensely relieved.

"Miss," warned Myaka, "telephone to States make much noise." He wiggled his fingers around his ears, indicating that the line was poor.

The call turned out to be a total disaster. Jeffrey was thoroughly put out that she had not shown up yet for the wedding. She gathered above the static on the line that several of his relatives from Michigan had flown down for the ceremony. When she told him between cracks and pops that her plane had gotten into trouble and that they had landed on a private island and were waiting for the plane to be repaired, he showed little concern for her safety. He nearly went berserk when she told him she didn't know when she would be able to get home. Then he asked her the name of the island but couldn't seem to get it straight. They were disconnected just as he began ranting at her for going to the Bahamas in the first place.

Nearly in tears, she walked back out onto the patio and plopped wearily in the chair beside Max, realizing that he had heard it all.

"He was upset. That's understandable," Max soothed. "He's disappointed."

Her chin trembled pathetically as she burst out angrily. "He's disappointed all right. Disappointed that I've inconvenienced his rotten relatives from Michigan. He didn't even ask if I was safe." A large crystalline tear slid down her small face, and she bit her lip viciously.

"Come along to your room," he urged. "You're tired and overwrought. We'll discuss it all after you get some rest."

"Aren't you going to say you're glad?" she flashed. "Aren't you going to say the marriage was a bad idea in the first place and it's a good thing it flopped?"

He led her into an enormous bedroom done in cool purples. "I wouldn't say anything at this time to make you more unhappy. This is no time to air my opinions on the subject."

"You didn't mind airing them before we took off from Nassau."

"That was when I thought you would be getting married tonight. Now I know you won't be. There's no point in rubbing salt in a wound, is there? Now get some rest. You're so tired, you're incapable of coherent thought."

He shut the door gently. She looked around and was immediately overwhelmed by the richness of her surroundings. A large round bed covered by a deep purple spread sat elegantly upon a dais. The walls of the room displayed a patterned paper of mingled purples threaded with gold.

Deep white carpeting completely muffled her footsteps as she walked across some distance to a bathroom in which was a lavender tub about the size of a small swimming pool, set in a glass alcove that looked out on a completely fenced in small tropical garden. Ponsonby certainly provided sumptuously for his guests. She wondered if he provided a lifeguard along with the tub. But it was only a quick shower she wanted. And bed. Upon further investigation she found a shower stall in a small hallway leading off from the bathroom. Here, there was also a private door leading to the outside.

She quickly undressed and opened the glass door to the stall. This was undoubtedly used by guests who wished to take a quick shower before or after a swim. She wondered fleetingly where Max's room was in this sprawling mansion and didn't doubt for a moment that he was as lavishly provided for as she.

After the shower she toweled off and put on a satin rust-colored nightie with a white lace bodice. She pulled back the heavy velvet spread, crawled between satin lavender sheets, and wondered how Jeffrey was managing to handle the situation at home.

The gilded French clock on the dresser showed seven. If things hadn't gone awry, she would be walking down the aisle about now. Poor Jeffrey. He would never forgive her for this. Mrs. Dunstan might not either. Weddings were costly. Buffy fervently hoped she hadn't gone to a lot of expense. It was to have been a small, private affair, but Jeffrey's mother tended to go overboard at times.

Well, at least they knew she was safe—that she hadn't had a terrible accident. Not that Jeffrey had seemed to care. Oh, it was all a mess. She sprawled under the cool sheets comfortably, and every bone in her body seemed to melt into a pool of relaxation.

Max had been so wonderful. He was a little overbearing at times, but really a prince. She drifted off into a deep sleep, smiling at the thought of Max's dark good looks, his penetrating gray eyes, not aware at all of the incongruity of dreaming of him instead of her fiancé. All thoughts of Jeffrey had fled her consciousness. And it didn't seem at all odd, for it happened frequently.

Later, she came slowly awake, taking her time to orient herself to her new surroundings. Moonlight filtered through the sheer draperies at the windows, and she remembered that she was on Ponsonby's Island. Throwing back the sheet, she padded across the huge room to peer at the clock. It was twenty after two. She had slept soundlessly for over seven hours.

She flipped the light on in the bathroom, doused her face over the sink, and decided that she was too wide awake to go back to bed.

She longed to go outside and take a walk in the lovely night air, but it wouldn't be polite to traipse through the house and risk waking Max and the two native servants at this hour.

Then she thought of the private door in her bathroom, which led to the outside. An amber light of mischief flickered in her clear brown eyes. Well, why not? A walk by the pool would be pleasant. And no one would be the wiser.

She opened the door and slipped soundlessly out into a warm, salt-tanged breeze laced delicately with the scent of blooming night jasmine. The walkway that led in the direction of the pool was lined with large oleander and rustling split-leaf philodendron. Bypassing the pool, she walked to the edge of the cliff.

33

A silver moon reflected itself on a silver sea. She stood entranced while these two elements of nature gently made love with one another.

After a few moments she came back to the pool and dipped her toe in experimentally. The water was tempting. Too tempting. A moonlight swim was what she wanted.

She cast a furtive glance around the large patio area, much of which was shrouded in shadows cast by lush tropical landscaping, bit her lips to keep from giggling, then pulled her nightie over her head and whisked off her brief panties, dropping them both carelessly on a lounge chair nearby.

What the heck, she thought as she slipped soundlessly into the water. They're all asleep.

"Beautiful," she breathed aloud before totally submerging her nubile body under the water. She played quietly, slicing arms and legs through the water soundlessly instead of splashing. When she tired of rolling and gliding in the water, she dove off the side several times, arching at just the right angle so that she would gracefully slide into the depths, barely creating a ripple.

"Oh, this is gorgeous," she whispered, surfacing and shaking her wildly curly head. "Thank you, Lord Ponsonby, wherever you are."

Then daringly reckless, she climbed upon the rocky waterfall at the far end of the kidney-shaped pool. The fountain that cascaded from it during the day had been turned off. She leaned back on her arms, exposing her softly feminine body to the silvering of the moonlight. It pearlized her smooth, shiny skin and contoured her curves.

Her silent communing with the elements was interrupted, however, by a strange aroma in the air. Cigar smoke! Sitting bolt upright, she peered into the philodendron not three yards away at poolside and saw the orange glow of a lit cigar.

"Eek!" She stood up in a flash and plummeted awkwardly into the water. With only her head exposed, she paddled over and grasped the side of the pool. A broadshouldered shadow lounged casually in a chair.

"Max?" she whispered fearfully.

"Yes?"

"How long have you been there?"

"Long enough."

"Oooh." She rested her forehead on the concrete between her hands as molten embarrassment coursed through her and flushed her in spite of the cold water. "Well, why didn't you say something," she hissed, turning to anger as a defense.

"And spoil your naughty play?" He moved forward, resting his arms on his knees.

She had the distinct impression that he was finding this incident amusing. Her anger mounted. "What are you anyway, some kind of damned voyeur?"

"Not at all. I couldn't sleep. I came here for the same reason you did. To take a swim. Although I did remember to dress for it," he added wickedly. "I didn't think you would take too kindly to my jumping in with you, so I decided to wait politely on the sidelines until you finished."

She knew he was laughing at her. The situation was intolerable. She longed to get out. The water was really getting chilly. But she couldn't possibly bring herself to rise out of the water like Aphrodite and saunter off nonchalantly to her room. She just couldn't let him see her like that, although she didn't know why now—he had already seen everything anyway.

He got up and came to where she clung to the side. She could see now that he wore light-colored swim trunks, and the superb view of his muscular legs did nothing to put her at ease.

"May I offer you a hand." He bent down, extending out his arm to her. She saw white teeth flashing clearly.

"Yes," she agreed on sudden impulse. "Thank you."

She allowed him to grasp her wrist securely, then pulled back with all her strength. He teetered on the edge for a moment, then gave up the balancing act in favor of making a belated, but graceful, dive into the pool.

Hauling herself out of the water in a frenzy, she made for her room, hoping to get out of sight before he surfaced. Her feet made little wet slapping noises against the deck as she ran.

It was only after she was behind her locked bathroom door that she allowed herself to breath. Good grief, what had she been thinking of to go skinny-dipping? She must have been moonstruck to even consider pulling such a stunt.

Her anger at her own folly mingled with anger toward him. Moving in spastic jerks, she toweled off and pawed around irritably in her luggage for her robe.

He should have spoken up, called out, coughed discreetly—something! Maybe he hadn't seen very much. After all, it was the middle of the night. No, the area had been flooded with moonlight. Those rocks particularly.

She flushed crimson, wrapped a terry robe around her trembling body, and tucked its lapels tightly across her soft, virginal breasts.

Turning on a tiny boudoir lamp, she sat at the dressing table and pulled viciously at her hair with a comb, accusing her reflection of being every kind of idiot.

How would she act when she saw him again? As if frolicking around naked was an everyday occurrence with her? Should she come right out and apologize? That would be even more embarrassing. Perhaps the best course would be not to mention it at all. To act as if it never happened.

She smelled food cooking, and her stomach complained loudly. Having eaten nothing since the chicken salad sandwiches, she suddenly felt almost sick with hunger. She sniffed her way to the door of her room but halted before opening it. Would it be Loa cooking at this hour? Had she awakened the whole house with her mad foolishness?

She identified the odors—bacon and eggs. And coffee. It was too much. She dressed quickly in a pair of green slacks and a sleeveless print blouse, being careful to button the blouse all the way up to her neck.

Walking into the kitchen, she saw Max standing over the stove, his hair still shining wetly from his recent dunking. He was fully but casually dressed in a pair of tan slacks and a brown short-sleeved shirt.

"I thought the smell of food would flush you out," he remarked as he heaped bacon, toast, and scrambled eggs onto a plate. He set it on the table and motioned her to sit down.

She obeyed, looking at the beautiful food and feeling suddenly quite nauseated, for hanging over the arm of the chair, neatly, was her nightie.

He placed a cup of coffee beside the plate and urged, "Go on. You must be starved. When I looked in on you earlier this evening, you were sleeping so soundly that I decided not to wake you for supper."

She stared at nothing, feeling the lump of nausea growing larger and larger. This disturbingly handsome man had seen her sleeping—and at the pool he had seen her as no other man had ever seen her before.

"I'm sorry," she mumbled thickly.

"Sorry?" He sat down beside her. "For what? For pulling me into the pool?" He chuckled deeply. "I expect a cold soak was just what I needed."

Buffy flushed to the roots of her blond curls as she looked shyly into his clear gray eyes, then quickly away.

"Don't be embarrassed," he spoke softly. "You make a lovely water nymph. It was a symphony. You're quite beautiful, you know."

"Don't say that," she trembled.

"Why not, when it's true? Eat your breakfast," he ordered calmly.

"Oh, I'm dumb." She shook her head. "It was careless and reckless of me to behave that way. What if the servants had seen?"

"Loa and Myaka have their own house down by the lagoon. They're only here during the day."

Buffy gasped, "You mean to tell me we're here alone!" She shoved her plate away and started to take flight.

"Sit down." He grabbed her wrist.

She looked directly into his lean, handsome face then and saw hard determination and glittering steel. What did he plan to do? She knew practically nothing about him. It was frightening. She sat down, not because he had ordered it, but because her legs felt as if they would no longer support her body.

"Now eat your food before it's ruined. You're quite safe with me. If I was planning to do you mischief, I would have already done so by now. You're engaged to be married. I'm not in the habit of poaching on another man's property."

"I'm sorry," she said again with an apologetic little smile. "I didn't mean to imply that you were not a gentleman."

"Yes, let's remember at all times that I am a gentleman," he said sarcastically as he leaned over and kissed a damp curl that had fallen over her forehead. "I shall deliver you to Jeffrey safe and sound."

"You are an honorable man," she teased, not realizing in the least how provocative she sounded.

"But of course."

He left abruptly then, Buffy imagined, to go to his room. It was late and he had not been to bed. She ate hungrily, cleaned up the kitchen, and sank back into bed herself just as the gray mist of predawn settled around the house.

Curling up in a kittenish fetal position, she thought of Max. She had known him only for a few hours, yet it seemed like an eternity. He really was a knight in shining armor. Her thoughts fragmented into the disconnected jumble that usually precedes sleep. Or a prince charming.

The next morning, Buffy met Loa in the kitchen and, sipping a cup of coffee, asked the whereabouts of Max.

"Gone lobstering, miss. We will have a fine supper tonight."

"If he comes in and asks where I am, will you tell him I've gone down to the beach?"

"Yes miss," Loa smiled.

Within half an hour she was on the beach, sunning lazily on a large beach towel in her white bikini. She had lived in Miami the past two years, not two miles from the ocean, yet hadn't been there more than a dozen times.

38

Most of her time was spent on the courts at Waterbrook, either practicing with Jeffrey or giving lessons. There hadn't been much time for fun and sun.

Staying in form for the tournaments she played was hard work. Quick dips in the olympic pool at the country club was the only relaxation she allowed herself during the day. Then at night she jogged with McMutt or went over to the Dunstans to watch television with Jeffrey.

Turning over on her stomach, she invited the tropical sun to warm her back as she frowned. Not a very exciting existence. Probably many women her age would think she lived a wildly glamorous life with all the traveling thither and yon to tournaments.

But it was hectic, and sometimes painful. The pressure of winning was sometimes excruciating. She invariably won, but the pressure of wondering if she would was something she bore all alone.

Even Jeffrey could offer her little more support at times; he went through his own private purgatories before a tournament.

There were times when she yearned with a longing almost beyond endurance for someone strong to lean on—something rocklike to anchor into. The Dunstans and Jeffrey were the closest she had come to finding that.

She wondered if Max had given any thought of how to get her to Miami. She sat up and looked around. A wave rolled peacefully into shore, leaving tinkling broken shells at its parting. A beautiful crop of tawny sea oats rustled behind her. The virginal sand around her was as fine and clean as sugar.

She crossed her legs in the lotus position and just breathed and absorbed the beautiful essences of Ponsonby's Paradise.

"Don't tell me you are a yogi as well as a tennis champion." Max's voice surprised her from behind.

She turned and saw him walking toward her in a pair of denim shorts. She wondered again how he kept so fit, for there was only lean, well-defined muscle under the bronze, hairy skin.

39

"I practice hatha-yoga to keep flexible." she confessed, wrinkling her nose at him. "It's beautiful here on this island." He sat down beside her. "I wish I could tuck a piece of it away somewhere inside me and take it back to so-called civilization." She unfolded her legs and began to rub them with suntan lotion.

"Do your back, too," he advised. "It's getting pink already. Don't you ever sun? You look as if you're wearing a white tennis dress instead of a white bikini. Only your arms and legs are tanned."

"I have no time for lying around in the sun," she answered. "Too busy giving lessons at Waterbrook and winning tournaments."

"Lie down and I'll do your back," he offered.

She turned over and as he rubbed her back with lotion, she mumbled thickly, "You know I could stay on this island lotus-eating for years, I think. Ponsonby must be a genius."

"As a matter of fact, I think you *should* stay on for a while, Buffy." He had begun to gently rub the lower part of her back. A strange and warm paralysis began to take over her body. "You need a rest," he went on. "You need time to think."

As his large capable hands dealt with the backs of her thighs, her mind lay stunned as the paralysis turned to a churning, tickling sensation.

She sat up on a quick indrawn breath.

"May I do your front?" he inquired politely.

"No!" she assured him quickly. "I can handle the front easily."

He rubbed excess lotion off his hands with her towel and looked at her directly, his eyes nearly silver in the bright sunlight. "Father won't be flying over for us. When I called him last night he was just about to fly out for our resort in Alberta. He thinks I deserve a week or two off, since I recently put so many hours in on that South Caicos deal. Our manager is quite capable of handling Palm Isle, so I'm staying here, Buffy, until the supply boat comes with the part for my plane."

40

"Where does that leave me?" she asked.

"Right here with me, I hope. I could call Nassau, of course, and hire a private plane to take you out. It would be costly. And with this airline strike, it would probably be tomorrow or the next day before they could work Ponsonby's Island into their schedule."

He lifted a shell and tossed it into the surf. "Frankly, I think you need time to relax and sort yourself out. Your fiancé also obviously needs a space—to get over his anger."

She hugged her knees under her chin and considered the problem. The wedding was ruined, and Jeffrey was angry. Rushing back at great expense and inconvenience to Max was not going to change that. Mr. Dunstan wouldn't appreciate her taking an unplanned vacation, on the other hand. But then, she must face the fact that all three Dunstans might never feel the same about her again after this.

She was not emotionally ready to face them and admittedly was not as sure about marrying Jeffrey as she had once been. Max was right. She did need time. The island was beautiful, and he was an exciting companion.

"Well?" he interrupted her thoughts. "What do you say?"

She turned a tanned, flawless face toward him and smiled. "You've got yourself a deal."

"I could kiss you for that." He laughed, obviously pleased with the arrangement.

"Oh, no you can't. You're a gentleman, remember? Besides, you wouldn't be able to catch me."

She raced down the beach in two skimpy white pieces of material—a lovely tousle-headed blond young woman whose feet barely touched the sand as she skimmed along, as free as the gulls that soared in the air above her.

CHAPTER 3

Lunch was an unexpected delight. They ate on the patio again, served by Loa. It was a meal of foods Buffy loved but was rarely able to enjoy, except when she made them for herself at home. A long-stemmed champagne glass was filled with fresh pineapple, oranges, and bananas, topped with a white creamy-looking dressing. Yogurt. What luxury! There were sandwiches made of whole grain bread, filled with paper-thin slices of cheese, green pepper, cucumber, and pimiento.

She watched furtively as Max ate. By now Jeffrey would be raising the roof, hollering for steak, hamburger, pork chops—anything more substantial. Jeffrey accused her of being a food fadist because she enjoyed fresh, whole foods rather than the greasy overcooked fare he preferred.

"Do you like this?" she inquired of Max hesitantly.

"Why, yes. Don't you?"

"Very much. But I sort of pictured you as a meat and potatoes man."

He raised a silver spoon dripping with fruit and yogurt to his mouth and ate with obvious pleasure. "Well, I'm not a man to turn down a good, lean steak, but in hot weather it's just a bit too heavy, don't you agree?"

"Yes." She watched him eat in fascination. "It's just that Jeffrey never touches yogurt and makes fun of me for loving it."

"One man's meat is another man's poison," he remarked with a twinkle in his eye. "Yogurt is a perfect food. Have you told Jeffrey that?"

"Oh, yes. But he is hooked on fast-food emporiums. You know—hamburgers, tacos, cardboard chicken." Max

43

smiled, wincing in mock sympathy. "We always have a summit conference about where to eat when we are away on tournaments."

"And you lose?" he asked, raising his brows.

"And I lose," she admitted. "It's a small thing, of course." She shrugged, nibbling at a sandwich.

"Since you are accustomed to eating whole foods, doesn't filling up on junk food at tournaments affect your performance?"

"It would, I'm sure, but I avoid eating when I'm with Jeffrey. I just wait until I'm some place where I can order what I want."

"If you marry the fellow, you could starve to death." His spoon rang melodiously against the crystal as he scooped out the last of his yogurt.

"I was hoping that after we were married I could sort of bring Jeffrey around to my way of thinking." She fished the slice of lime out of her empty tea glass and began eating it. "How does Loa make such delicious iced tea?" Loa, who had just come out with their coffee, smiled at her.

Max smiled too. "That's risky business."

Buffy looked at him questioningly. "Tea?" she asked.

"No. Trying to remake a man after marriage. It can be very frustrating and almost always ends in failure."

Buffy, sensing an impending lecture, remarked, "It's a small matter. We are compatible in every other way."

"Really?" he asked as if he didn't believe it for a moment. He sipped his coffee, piercing her with his keen silver gaze.

"Yes," she averred stoutly.

He set his coffee cup down and stretched languorously, every muscle in his chest seeming to ripple under his thin silky shirt. "Buffy," he yawned, "you are as lovely as a wild fawn, but as stubborn as a nanny goat."

She stiffened angrily. "Just what is that supposed to mean? One doesn't break off an engagement over yogurt, you know!"

He chuckled sleepily, "What, then?"

"I-I don't know," she stammered uncomfortably. "But certainly not over one's eating habits."

"You're quite intelligent; yet sometimes you're frightfully stupid," he mused, looking at her from heavy-lidded eyes.

"You're insulting me again," she drawled menacingly, "and I don't like it."

"Sorry." He got up, stretched again, and said, "I'm for a little siesta. How about you?"

"Is that a proposition?" she cooed, despising his arrogance and purposely trying to put him off guard.

His firm, chiseled mouth went into a smile as he leaned over the table, his warm, regular breathing fanning her face. "No." He studied her face with teasing uncertainty. Then, aiming at a spot under her delicately molded cheekbone, he sleepily kissed it, murmuring, "Unfortunately."

She watched him saunter off to his room with easy grace, and her face flamed with angry embarrassment. He was always so cool, always in such control, always ready to show her up for a stupid, ignorant child. His strength and self-possession galled her, yet drew her in some fascinating way. What would it be like to see a man like Max fall apart? Something like watching Samson pull down the pillars in the temple. She shuddered, wondering what sort of woman could bring a man like Max to his knees. Indeed, she doubted if such a woman existed.

For all of his talk about falling madly in love, she seriously doubted that he would ever condescend to do so himself. He was obviously a man of the world—a man who could favor any woman with a debonair, impersonal kiss as he had just done to her, then walk off completely untouched by it. She smiled inwardly. Yes, Max would most certainly offer some woman of the world a marvelous challenge. Buffy knew her limits—taking on a man like Max was definitely not within them.

"More coffee, miss?" Loa asked at her elbow.

"No, thank you, but I would like another glass of tea, I think."

Loa poured her another glass and Buffy helped herself to a slice of lime from a nearby silver bowl.

"How do you make such clear, luscious tea?" she asked the servant.

"Honey," Loa said. "A spoonful mixed in while it is still warm. Touch of honey make tea better." She smiled openly at Buffy and commented, "That is what you look like, miss."

"What?" Buffy asked uncomprehendingly.

"You look like honey, miss, with that gold hair and those pretty light-brown eyes. Even your skin is golden. I never before see anyone with your color." She smiled at Buffy shyly.

Buffy realized that she must indeed look unusual to the satiny black Loa. "Well, thank you for the compliment." She laughed. "And thank you for the beautifully prepared lunch."

They fell into a conversation on the science of making yogurt, Buffy keenly questioning the older woman on how long she cooked it and the ingredients she used. She helped to clear the table and to wash up the dishes amid protests from the nervous servant, who seemed to have never before been treated with such equality by a guest. Finally Loa relaxed as she began to warm under Buffy's friendly chatter and obvious disinclination to observe class distinctions.

"Does Mr. Shepherd come here often to vacation?" she asked Loa conversationally as she dried silverware.

"He come not too often," she spoke.

Buffy noticed that Loa's voice was deeply alto, and although she spoke with better sentence structure than Myaka, she often left out words or misplaced them, which was charming and altogether intelligible.

"He is a busy man," Buffy observed.

"He busy, he work much, he very nice man," Loa strung out rather disjointedly. "I make good food for him when he come here. My man and me, we like Mr. Shepherd very much. He look after our two sons on Nassau. See they good and fine."

46

"Two sons? That's wonderful."

"They are Pelo and Lucay," Loa put in proudly. "They go to school on New Providence Island. We see them on holidays and in summer. We miss them very much. But Mr. Shepherd, he look out for them."

"I see." Buffy raised her brows and tilted her head thoughtfully. Max was a sort of godfather figure to the two boys, she supposed.

"He teach them to play tennis. Boys stay busy—keep out of trouble."

"Max plays some amateur tennis?" She took in this new bit of information like a predator sniffs the scent of fresh prey.

Loa, not having the remotest idea of the meaning of the word amateur, nodded eagerly.

"Well, well, will wonders never cease," Buffy mused. How she would like to play Max and flatten him thoroughly. She grinned wickedly as she imagined the sweet success of the kill.

"I think I'll go down to the beach for a while, Loa." She flipped her dish towel over the rack and bounced out of the kitchen energetically.

"You be careful," Loa warned, rolling her black eyes balefully. "Too much sun ruin your pretty skin."

"I will," Buffy coughed heading for her room to change.

Before going down on the beach, she made a tour of the immediate grounds around Ponsonby's large sprawling house. Beyond a small grove of pine trees she encountered a beautiful sight—a tennis court. She ran onto the green surface gleefully. Before leaving Ponsonby's Paradise she would get the arrogant Max Shepherd into a match. She rubbed her hands together in malicious anticipation.

He had such a mastery of everything in his world. He was so superior with his knowing silver-sheened eyes and easy, yet lordly, bearing. But this small expanse of hard surface bisected by innocent white net was her domain—the one place in the world where she was in control. She

47

tapped it lovingly with her foot. Oh, it would be a great day for womankind when she trounced Max decisively on the court. She would be ruthless, unmerciful. It was the least she could do—and probably all she could do.

Loa's generous warning completely fled her mind as she walked into the deep sand of Ponsonby's beach. The water, sparkling with lazy glinting waves, danced in the late September sunshine. The warm hypnotic breeze blowing up from it lulled her into a mindless, worriless state.

She knew the sun in Florida could burn year round, but neglected to reason that the same must certainly hold true in this even more tropical location. And, as is often the case, it was already too late when she realized her folly.

It was not until after she had showered and begun dressing for dinner that she realized just how much sun she had gotten. Her back was tender and sensitive. Fingerprints showed white, then flamed to scarlet everytime she touched her shoulder.

A girl from Florida should have known better. Twenty minutes to half an hour was more than enough time to expose virgin skin to tropical sun. She had been out there at least three hours, and realized now that she had a first-class sunburn—the kind that made sleeping comfortably impossible and resulted eventually in hundreds of blisters followed by dry, unattractive peeling.

Well, the damage was done. The longer she stood before the mirror examining it, the redder it seemed to glow. She chose a loose-fitting print dress of a synthetic fiber to wear, thinking its looseness would make her more comfortable. The very idea of wearing a bra and hose nearly nauseated her, so she cast them aside.

After applying some eye shadow and lipstick, blusher not being necessary, she took a look at herself. Her face and arms were more gloriously golden than ever, her hair, more blond. Wincing, she got up to go to the dining room. It was only her back and stomach that hurt and stung. And the loose-fitting dress had been a poor choice after all, its synthetic fiber refusing to breath. The heat coming off her roasted torso was trapped against her like molten armor.

There was a knock at the door and Loa's soft voice: "Dinner, miss."

"I'll be there in a jiffy," she called through the door. Straightening, then wiping little beads of perspiration from her upper lip with unsteady fingers, she made her way to the dining room.

Loa had set the table beautifully. The fine china and stemware glistened under an even more glittering chandelier. Polished silver gleamed on white lace. Red hibiscus and candles formed a rich-looking centerpiece.

"Oh, Loa, it's beautiful," she admired. Loa received the compliment with her usual shy smile.

"Did you enjoy your siesta?" she asked Max as he seated her at the table.

"Ah, yes, I'm quite rested now," he answered, taking a place opposite her. "Loa tells me you spent the afternoon on the beach. I hope you didn't get too much sun. I think our sun here in the islands is even hotter than yours in Florida."

She shifted herself gingerly. Loa brought in a fresh fruit cup and she began eating mechanically. "As a matter of fact, I did get a wee bit too much on my back."

"Oh?" He was immediately concerned. "I hope you're not too uncomfortable."

"No, no," she lied brightly. "It's not that bad." She shifted again in her chair and focused her attention on Loa, who was bringing in a huge platter of stuffed lobsters.

The delicious dinner momentarily took her mind off the seething skin underneath her dress. The lobsters were cooked to moist, fleshy perfection; the stuffing was spicy and tasty; and the little baby squash and mushroom buttons baked in a cheese sauce were like nothing she had ever tasted before.

She and Max talked easily. He described how he caught the lobster and suggested she go with him one morning. He also told her that the fresh vegetables and fruit were grown on the island in a garden spot on the high fertile

49

hill behind Loa and Myaka's house above the lagoon. Also, Ponsonby had a huge walk-in freezer, where he kept beef, pork, out-of-season vegetables, bread, and even milk in a frozen state. When she inquired about the power on the island, Max explained that Lord Ponsonby had a huge generator, which took care of it all. Ponsonby's Paradise was really a utopia.

Max plied Buffy with a delicious French wine the whole time they talked, and by the end of the meal she felt replete and utterly uninhibited. She talked brightly, not feeling at all ill at ease as she sometimes did with Jeffrey.

Both Max and Jeffrey were incredibly chauvinistic. Buffy secretly suspected that all men were, by and large, no matter what liberated views they claimed to have. When Jeffrey dominated her it made her feel somewhat like an ancient, stupefied mummy.

On the other hand, Max's high-handed behavior toward her had the opposite effect: she felt stimulated, alive in his company. Even when he made her angry it was a reaction of intense awareness to him. Max's male domination whipped all her senses to an elevated level. It was impossible to be indifferent to him. There wasn't a dull molecule in his body. And there seemed to be a strange chemistry within her, as old as life itself, which responded to him.

He had a liqueur after dinner in a tiny long-stemmed gold goblet. She refused his offer of some, at which time he asked Loa to bring her another glass of wine.

She covered her glass with her hand and wrinkled her nose reproachfully. "Max, I've already had two glasses. I'm not used to it."

"Nonsense. Another glass. It has colored you beautifully," he teased with light-gray eyes that danced like the waves upon a silver summer sea.

It was true. The wine had made her already warm body glowingly flushed. It had loosened her tongue to a degree of charming giddiness. She was totally enjoying herself in the company of this exciting man. And as long as she was careful not to move too quickly or sit back in her seat abruptly, the sunburn was not too painful.

"Max?" She leaned over to speak with him conspiratorially. He leaned toward her, too, smiling into her liquid-gold eyes indulgently. "Are you trying to get me drunk?"

"Heaven forbid." He held up a hand with pretended seriousness. "I merely wish to see you have a good time." He quickly kissed her retroussé nose.

"Well, then, you're terrifically successful. I can't remember ever having had a more enjoyable time." She cupped her chin in her palm and looked at him gratefully.

He took her hand from her face. "I'm glad, Buffy." She gave a little breathless gasp as he kissed her palm.

Each hour with Max was drastically altering the course of her life. She didn't understand it, but she knew she would never be the same again after being here in this island paradise with Max Shepherd.

He got up, sat his empty goblet on the stereo, and put on an album, filling the room with soft, gorgeous mood music. She should have been wary, should have been nervous. But she was neither. The island was romantic, Max was wonderful; the wine had apparently done its work. She got up and held out her arms to him, challenging, teasing, and for a moment, totally surrendering to him.

"Dance with me, Max," she whispered.

A brief, unreadable expression swept across his face, replaced quickly by urbane politeness. "But of course." He reached out, pulling her almost roughly into his arms, and she cried out in pain.

He could feel the heat from her back coming through her clothes and pushed her away to look at her half in anger, half in pity. "You're really sunburned, aren't you? A few times tonight I saw you wincing as if in pain."

"It's not too bad. It will turn into a tan tomorrow."

He put his hand on her back again, and she gasped as she shrank under his touch.

"Not too bad, you say? Let me see," he demanded. "Unzip."

"No!" But before she could move away he reached one hand behind her and deftly unzipped her dress. He obvi-

51

ously knew how to handle women's clothing as well as everything else.

"Turn around, let me see." he ordered.

She turned around slowly and reluctantly. He gingerly pulled the opening a little wider and she heard a hissing sound come from between clenched teeth.

"It's a wonder you didn't feel cannibalistic eating lobster tonight. You look like one." He touched her back very gently and whistled. "Is it this bad just on your back?"

"Yes, my back is the worst. My stomach and . . . er . . . chest are burnt, too. But not as bad."

"There's still quite a bit of heat in the skin. I think we could fry an egg on your back."

She laughed hollowly. "I should have been more careful," she apologized, turning to him. "I do know how treacherous the sun is even when it feels merely warm." She looked down miserably. "You must really think I'm a child."

"I do at that." He chuckled, forcing her to look into his compelling eyes. "A beautiful child, with one heck of a sizzling sunburn." He held her chin between his thumb and forefinger. "But I know some magic for it."

She pulled her gaze away from his, not doubting for a moment that he was some kind of fantastic magician.

"Loa," he called.

"Yes," answered the servant, who appeared immediately at the door of the dining room, wiping her hands on a dish towel.

"Get us some aloe, please. Miss Vallentine will have to be given our special treatment for sunburn."

"Yes, sir," Loa replied, hurrying away only to come back momentarily with a tray of long, spearlike leaves.

"Lie down on the couch, Buffy," he instructed.

She looked from Loa to Max uncertainly, feeling somewhat like a guinea pig.

"Go on, girl," he urged. "The aloe is a marvelous medicine for burns. Loa and Myaka introduced it to me several years ago when I came here on vacation and spent too much time water skiing under a blazing summer sun."

Buffy slowly lay down, her dress making a profusion of wildly exotic flowers around her as she exposed her back to him. "What are you going to do?"

"Rub you down with aloe sap," he answered. "I promise it will take the heat out of your back and keep you from blistering."

She watched Loa slit each round, fleshy leaf from top to bottom. A clear sticky fluid oozed out. Max picked up one of these leaves and opened it to expose this liquid even more, then gently rubbed it across her shoulders.

She flinched at first, but the flesh of the plant slid over her seething skin so coolly that she found herself relaxing and actually enjoying it.

Loa smiled at her indulgently. "Aloe good medicine. We use it much here in the islands." The servant then left the room for other parts of the house, as if having Max doctor the bare back of a girl lying prostrate on Ponsonby's lush white couch was an everyday occurrence.

"Loa doesn't seem shocked at all by this procedure," Buffy commented.

"Natives are marvelously uninhibited," he explained. "Nakedness does not shock them. To them it is a natural state."

Buffy nestled her stomach and breasts into the tropical flowers of her dress more firmly, seeking there absolute camouflage.

Apparently Max noticed this defensive movement, for he commented with a certain wickedness, "As a matter of fact, Loa is probably wondering why you and I don't sleep together."

"Max!" she gasped.

He chuckled richly. "Loa and Myaka lived together seven years before finally being married by a priest over on Nassau a few years ago. They had already had two sons. To natives, making love is something one does naturally."

"But it's promiscuous," she protested.

"Not at all," he argued in clipped British tones. "Your dress has to come down a little more, Buffy," he said,

53

unzipping it to the panty line. He smeared the aloe down her slim, taut back to the hollow where her waist met her hips, then moved it gently around the very tender area where she had been burned the worst.

"Loa and Myaka are very devoted to one another," he went on to explain. "Theirs was a beautiful marriage even before it became legal. A lot less hypocritical than many of our so-called civilized marriages, where everything is properly legal but completely devoid of true love, don't you think?"

"Their culture is different from ours." She knew he was using Loa and Myaka's love to stab home a point about her and Jeffrey's lack of it. It made her angry that he insisted on meddling in this matter at every opportunity.

"Ah, yes. More primitive perhaps, but yet in some ways more honest than our civilized one."

"I hope you're not an advocate of cohabitation," she spoke tensely. "I think it is a despicable cop-out."

"I think it is a cop-out, too." She could not see, but could sense, his smug smile. "I do not believe in two people living together irresponsibly. But neither do I believe in two people living together legally when there isn't a particle of real love between them."

"You're talking about me and Jeffrey again," she burst out furiously. She lunged off the couch, clutching her draping, dangerously slipping dress about her fiercely.

One side of his well-molded mouth lifted in a sardonic half-smile of admission.

"You damned know-it-all," she hurled at him before stomping out of the room in a rage.

She slammed her bedroom door so hard that it vibrated alarmingly on its hinges. Throwing off her dress, she thrust herself into her terry robe, unmindful of the pain it caused, uttering several unladylike imprecations that must have been clearly audible through the door and beyond.

He opened the door softly, and quietly walked into the room. She cut herself off in the middle of one very scathing sentence. He set the tray of aloe leaves on the dresser.

"Doctor your stomach with these," he ordered. Her eyes

opened wide as he unbuttoned his shirt and pulled it out of his pants. He shrugged out of the white garment, which was made of the thin muslin-like material so much in style. "Wear this instead of that heavy robe. I expect you back out in the living room in five minutes. You still owe me a dance."

His broad naked back rippled as he turned and arrogantly strode out of the room, closing the door with a firm click.

She reached for a lavender velvet pillow on the bed and in an uncontrollable fit of pique, threw it at the door with all her strength. It made a muffled poofing noise as it hit the wood, falling soundlessly to the thick carpeting below—symbolic of how effectual her anger was against him.

He came back through the door and walked up to her, totally self-possessed. "You have a very nasty temper, my child. I've been meaning to speak to you about it."

"Don't you 'my child' me, you pompous oaf!" she flashed.

He placed his hands on his hips, baring to her view every well-cut muscle in his chest and stomach. "I shall have to spank you if you don't curb it," he mused softly in his well-modulated British accent.

She gulped, visibly intimidated. "You wouldn't dare. You are a gentleman," she reminded him.

"And as such, I don't take kindly to being spoken to in terms that would burn the ears off a sailor. Now, mind your tongue," he warned nicely, "or I will give you a lesson that will encourage you to speak like a proper lady in the future."

Buffy bit her lip to hold back the several colorful things she wanted to say to him. She did this with difficulty, since controlling her runaway temper was not one of her few redeeming virtues. "I don't like being threatened," she finally was able to remark acidly. "And I have never been spanked. You'd better not ever try it, you—" She clamped her lips shut against calling him something that would cast definite disparagement upon his lordly parentage.

"I assure you," he averred politely, "if the occasion

55

arises, I shall thrash you soundly. Without compunction. I don't know what sort of upbringing one gets in an orphanage, but by all indications, yours left a lot to be desired."

"They did their best," she put in hotly, defending Mr. Johnson, his plump, kindly wife, and the various house mothers who had been in charge of her during her several years at the orphanage.

"And what did they do, Buffy, when you needed discipline?" he asked.

"They took away our television privileges, or our desserts," she answered.

"Never a good, sound spanking administered with a firm, loving hand?"

"Of course not," she said exasperatedly. "Corporal punishment was not in the policy."

"What a pity. I'm sure you must have needed it often."

She turned away from him, highly incensed, yet sensible enough to realize that he was not bluffing. A new emotion was added to the several she already felt toward him—fear. Max was a man to be feared and respected. She could not get by with mouthing off to him like she did to Jeffrey and her tennis buddies, sometimes shocking them with one or two well-turned phrases.

"I'll be out directly," she promised him as sweetly as she could.

"Very well. I'll be waiting." His deeply timbred voice still hung in the air after he had left.

She swabbed the cooling aloe over her chest and stomach, eased into fresh underclothes, then put on Max's shirt. It smelled of lime after-shave, and a faint tang of cigar smoke still clung to it—a surprisingly pleasant mixture.

She carried the tray of used aloe leaves to the kitchen. Loa must have already left for home, for the kitchen was brightly tidy. After depositing the tray on the counter, she walked into the living room haltingly, feeling incongruously shy in the aftermath of her confrontation with him. His loose shirt hung to her knees, not transparent, yet sub-

56

tly suggestive of the slim but well-rounded figure underneath.

"Not exactly a ball gown," she apologized with a little laugh.

"It will do very nicely." Having changed into another shirt, he stood by the bar and tossed down a shot of whiskey.

She swallowed thickly as she recognized the music that floated tremulously through the air from the stereo—"Strangers in the Night."

He walked toward her, taking her lightly into his arms. And they danced. It was slow, lazy dancing during which she moved progressively closer to him in spite of herself until her cheek brushed across his chest, then lay there dreamily.

Carefully avoiding her sunburn, he rested his large hand on her hip. They danced together in perfect synchronization. There was a lovely molecular harmony between them that they dared not analyze.

"Thank you for not touching my sunburn," she whispered.

"I am a polite man," he spoke into her curls.

"I'm sorry I lost my temper with you."

"All is forgiven."

"Mr. J. threatened to spank me several times when I was a child, but he knew it was against the rules."

"Mr. J.?"

"We all called him Mr. J.—Mr. Johnson is his name. He is the director of the orphanage. He and his wife sort of took me under their wing."

"I see. And you gave Mr. J. a hard time, I take it."

"It was my temper which always got me into trouble. Mr. J. was always quoting scripture to me about it. He is a minister. I grew up in a Baptist-sponsored orphanage."

"I do hope you didn't deliver Mr. Johnson the sort of sermon you gave me awhile ago."

"No. I didn't learn to do that until after I left the orphanage. I *am* sorry, Max."

"Shhh," he whispered, pulling her closer.

"Max?"

"Hmm?"

"You wouldn't really spank me, would you?"

She heard a low rumbling chuckle in his chest. "Don't try me, girl."

"Max," she breathed slowly, knowing then without a doubt that he would certainly take her in hand if she allowed her temper to run rampant again.

Another chuckle began in his chest and erupted into an outright laugh. "You do string out my name. Maaaaax . . ." he drawled in bad imitation.

"Well, it's better than your quick British 'Boofy.' "

He threw back his dark masculine head and laughed delightedly. "You're a minx. A beautiful, lovable minx."

CHAPTER 4

The next morning, before sunrise, Buffy woke to an insistent knocking at her bedroom door.

"Buffy, wake up," Max called.

Immediately alert, she tumbled out of bed, shrugged into her robe, and opened the door.

"Would you like to go lobstering with me?" he asked her without preamble. He stood before her, negligently handsome in a pair of dark swim trunks and a casual pullover shirt.

"Y-yes," she stammered. "I'd love to."

"Meet me in the kitchen in ten minutes." He turned to go. "And wear something over that tiny white bathing costume. I don't want you to get any more sun on your back today."

"Okay," she agreed, closing the door.

She decided to put on her red tennis dress over the bathing suit. Loa kept her clothes laundered and her room tidy to a ridiculous degree. Every time Buffy took off a garment, then came back to look for it, she found that the phantom Loa, on one of her frequent plundering visitations, had collected everything even faintly resembling dirty laundry. This tennis dress, now bright and fresh, was the one she was afraid would molder in the plastic bag at the bottom of her suitcase.

She laughed silently as she groomed herself in the mirror. Not very fashionable to go lobstering in a tennis dress; but, then, neither was it the rage to go dancing in an oversized man's white shirt. Max wouldn't expect her to look like a fashion plate anyway. She realized he must

59

consider her an impish child. His threatening to spank her had proven that.

She snorted aloud, half in anger, half in awe, as she made her way to the kitchen.

They ate a delicious breakfast he had expertly prepared. When he began to clear the table she protested with faint sarcasm, "I'll do it. I'm not totally helpless, you know."

"Sometimes I wonder," he remarked, sitting down to a second cup of coffee.

She threw the silverware into the sink with more force than necessary. "You're the first person I've ever met who isn't impressed by how independent I am." She ran hot water in the sink and squirted in liquid soap simultaneously. "Most all my friends think Little Orphan Annie has come a long way. After all, I'm capable of traveling anywhere on my own. And I'm somewhat famous, although certainly not rich."

"You're abysmally immature," he said blandly. "Allowing yourself to get into an engagement with Dunstan proves it."

She scrubbed plates viciously, realizing prudently that telling Max off again could only prove disastrous. "That's your opinion," she finally cooed.

He got up and walked over to empty his cup into the sink. Then he took up a towel and began to dry dishes.

"Isn't it amazing," she blinked sweetly, "how you male chauvinists are always trying to prove how liberated you are by doing little housewifely things like drying a few lousy teacups."

"Oh, please," He gave a sardonic laugh. "Let's don't get into women's liberation. You females always resort to it when backed into a corner. Your very harping on it proves only too clearly that you are aware of the natural domination of the male species and are adolescently resentful of our authority," he jibed.

She gave him a wide, smoldering stare and wrung out her dish rag fiercely. "You're forgetting the black widow spider. I wouldn't say that the male in that case fares too well. All he gets for his efforts at domination is a good

60

swift sting. After which he throws up his furry little legs and dies." She slung the rag into the now empty sink with a resounding thud.

He threw back his dark handsome head and laughed delightedly. "You are quite a little fighter, aren't you? One way or the other you manage to have your say."

"I've had to be tough," she admitted shortly. "I wouldn't be where I am today if I weren't. Not everybody is born with a silver spoon in his mouth."

"So, you are also an inverted snob," he accused with a deadly smile. "You resent very much that I was born heir to a title and quite wealthy. I suppose you think I'm a spoiled layabout who has never worked a day in his life."

"No." She looked down, feeling suddenly ashamed. "I don't think that, really."

He slipped his arm around her shoulder easily. "Come on," he urged gently. "Standing here arguing with you, as stimulating as it is, will not catch us any lobsters."

They made their way down to the boathouse where Ponsonby's motorboat was moored, Max's arm still slung negligently around her shoulders.

"How's the sunburn today?" he asked.

"It doesn't hurt at all. Thank you for doctoring it."

"It was my pleasure." He untied the boat and helped her get in.

Ponsonby's boat was a sleek mackerel-green inboard, which sported a canvas awning over the control section and the two back-to-back double seats.

"Lord Ponsonby uses this to go grouper fishing," Max explained. "The grouper in these waters are magnificent and not at all as played out as they are in your Florida waters."

"It's a nice boat," she observed. "Don't you grouper fish?"

"Sometimes. But I'm fond of lobstering. Grouper are heavy, sluggish creatures. One has to pull a grouper up from the depths like a lead weight. Lobsters, on the other hand, for all their horny spikes and cumbersome appear-

61

ance, are cagey, and it takes quite a nimble hand to catch them."

He started the motors, which purred like sleeping tigers in their built-in boxes, then expertly pulled the boat out of its little house.

The water was a slate, glassy gray in the early morning haze. Buffy wrapped her arms around her body, suddenly chilled in the moist, salty air.

"Cold?" he asked with eyes as calmly gray as the water that surrounded them. When she nodded he dredged into a canvas duffel bag he'd brought along and pulled out a crumpled red Windbreaker. He then idled the motor while he placed the jacket around her shoulders solicitously.

"There," he smiled. "Better?"

She nodded again, wondering at his inevitable concern for her. But wasn't Max always the proper gentleman? Always the knight in shining armor? Always the self-possessed male—touched, yet untouchable?

He threw the boat ahead full speed toward a horizon that was rapidly streaking with orange, vermilion, and lavender slashes.

Finally he cut the motor, threw out an anchor, and pulled his shirt over his head. "This looks like a likely spot," he announced, going over to peer into the water.

Buffy watched him silently as he moved to sort out some tackle. The growing dawn burnished his dark hair, giving it a bronze, fiery shine. A golden glow lay over his powerfully built shoulders and caressed his clean-shaven jawline. He fascinated her; he didn't seem a reality.

"Have you ever used a snorkel?" he asked.

She jumped involuntarily. "No."

"No matter. You'll catch on fast." He shuffled his feet into fins. "You swim very well."

She blushed furiously, remembering how he'd discovered that fact.

He put on a mask and a snorkel, then poised himself on the side of the boat. "Don't go away," he said before going over the side.

"I won't," she promised feebly to the empty spot where he'd been.

He stayed down an indeterminably long time. She went to the side and peered down into about fifteen feet of clear water, which was growing more and more crystalline in the early morning sunlight.

He surfaced about five yards away, blowing a spurt of water out of the snorkel, then dove again, silently cutting the water like a sleek porpoise.

Eventually he scaled the side of the boat and threw two orangeish-brown, spiny lobsters onto the deck before climbing aboard.

"They're down there all right." He laughed.

She walked over to the two absolutely gruesome-looking creatures in all their spiky glory and made an instant resolution that she would have nothing to do with any of their kind unless they were safely ensconced on a well-garnished dinner platter.

"Ready to try your luck?" He grinned.

One of them made a little kicking gesture toward her with all of its several legs and she stepped back instantly, thoroughly intimidated.

"There's nothing to it, really," he went on. "I catch them with my bare hands. But I wouldn't suggest that for a novice. They're quite prickly, as you can see."

"Max," she began, "I don't think—"

"You will use a net and prod," he cut her off, either oblivious to her reluctance or deliberately ignoring it. He slid out of his fins and rummaged around in the tackle, selecting her gear. Mask, fins, and snorkel sailed through the air and landed at her feet. Then he held up what appeared to be a butterfly net and a golfing iron minus the head.

"Now, let me explain the procedure," he said pedantically, taking a seat opposite her. "The lobster is a creature who, during the day, rests beneath the water behind rocks and ledges. He is abominably stupid, because, like the ostrich, he considers his position well hidden. Actually his long, very noticeable antennae invariably project out into plain view."

63

Buffy looked distastefully at the two creatures on the deck and shuddered as they demonstrated their long, writhing projections accommodatingly. She cleared her throat and opened her mouth to speak, but Max cut in explaining,

"Now, when the clever lobster catcher sees a pair of these antennae, he goes up and prods said lobster gently in the side. Gently, mind you, or—"

"Or the vicious little devil will dart out and snap off a hand, I'll bet," Buffy burst out.

He laughed. "No, no, Buffy. They're timid creatures when up against man. If you prod them too roughly, they merely scuttle away, and you've lost a good catch. Floridian and Bahamian lobsters are really a type of crayfish. They don't even have claws. Haven't you noticed?"

She looked closely and saw that indeed they didn't possess huge snapping claws. Somehow this gave her little comfort.

"Do they bite?" she asked.

"No." He gave a deep, rich laugh that proved her suspicion that he was having some fun at her expense. "All you have to do is give a lobster a little tickle and he'll swim right into your net. I promise."

"You don't really expect me to go down there armed with only that flimsy net and a decapitated golf club, do you?"

"Why not? You're the one always boasting of blood and guts. I thought this would be a piece of cake to one as tough as you claim to be."

It was a challenge she could not ignore. She silently put on her gear, then lumbered over to the edge of the boat, arranging herself precariously on the side of it.

"Now, be sure to blow the water out of your snorkel when you surface, or you might get badly strangled."

She rolled her eyes balefully from behind the mask, vowing silently that she would murder him on the tennis courts if it was the last thing she ever did.

As she went over the side she heard him laugh a warning that sounded like "Look out for Jaws."

She bobbed to the surface immediately, peering through her mask for a big, voracious, toothy maw bearing down upon her. Max was really having a field day.

After paddling around slowly for a few minutes though, she nearly forgot about him as the wonder and beauty of what she was seeing completely captivated her. There were bright corals and even brighter finger sponges, flowing brown and ochre ribbons of seaweed undulated as if in an underwater breeze, and myriads of tiny metallic fish darting helter-skelter. She reached down and tried to grab one of these shining live jewels, but it made a quick feint and was gone.

She dove down into this new world and swam around in awe in its silent crystal air. After staying down as long as she could, she soared to the surface, breaking through its mirrored ceiling with a gasp. But she did not blow all the water out of the snorkel in her greed for oxygen, and strangled.

Max was suddenly at her side, holding her, tearing off her mask and snorkel as she coughed and spluttered.

"I knew you would do that," he said, holding her up as he treaded water with his strong, muscular legs.

"Oh, Max!" she choked, drawing in great gulps of air. "It's beautiful down there. I-it's absolutely fantastic down there."

"Are you all right?" he asked, drawing her closer.

"Oh, I'm fine." She grabbed for her mask and snorkel eagerly. "It's like another world—a world of shimmering jewels and diamond bubbles."

"Are you sure you're okay?"

"Yes, yes," she assured him. "Come on," she urged. "Let's just swim along on the surface for a while and look."

With the net and prod in one hand and Max's strong fingers in the other, she swam lazily and silently along with him as fish frolicked beneath them in watery green sunbeams.

He pointed down at some rocks. She saw two wicked

head out of the water and forced her to come up, too. antennae waving contrary to the current. He pulled his

"Well, there's your first lobster. Go to it."

She shoved her mask to the top of her head and looked doubtful.

"Go on, go on. Don't keep him waiting. Don't tell me you're going to let a little eight-inch, clawless crayfish get the best of you."

She bravely rearranged her mask, took a deep breath, and dove. Tentatively approaching the rock, she held out the net with one hand and eased the prod in the general vicinity of the animal's body with the other. Surprised and utterly exultant, she watched the bronzish, ugly thing scurry right into the net. There was a moment of intense madness as she grappled with her tools and the squiggling prey. She finally managed to choke the net with a vengeful hand just before soaring upward. She broke through the surface, blowing water out of her snorkel with great force.

Spitting the snorkel out of her mouth, she laughed. "I got it! Max, I got it!"

He took her net and held up the ugly prize. "I knew you would. Let's go back to the boat now."

"But aren't we going to catch more lobsters?" she protested excitedly, completely unaware of how incongruous her present eagerness was to her previous reluctance.

He smiled. "Yes, after we have something to eat and drink. I packed us some sandwiches and iced tea in the duffel."

"Do you always think of everything?"

"Invariably."

She hoisted herself agilely to the side of the boat, looking like some awful, mutated mermaid in her red tennis dress. Max threw her lobster beside the others, and she noted with satisfaction that it was the largest.

He handed her a towel and began to rub down his neck and chest while she scrubbed her blond salty curls vigorously.

"Oh, that was fun! I can't wait to go back in."

He held his towel in midair and then began to mop his own head slowly. "I wonder at times, my girl, if you've ever had a bit of fun in your life."

She looked at him painfully, all the sorrow of her loveless, lonely childhood standing in her liquid-amber eyes. "Don't pity me, Max."

"I wouldn't dream of it." He fished a sandwich out of the bag and handed it to her with ceremony. "How does one pity a well-wrapped, but very volatile, package of dynamite? I admire you very much."

She took the proffered sandwich with a wry smile, disbelieving that he held her in any kind of esteem at all.

During the rest of the morning, they ate the sandwiches, drank out of the same Thermos, and caught twenty-four lobsters, Buffy catching her fair share of them. The sun grew hotter; the boat bobbed and curtsied in sapphire swells. Buffy lost all sense of time as she released herself into a pleasurable world ruled only by Max.

He cleverly got her to divulge her real first name—a closely guarded secret. Having the name Bernadine was the bane of her existence. Max agreed that it was pretty bad and didn't at all suit her like Buffy. He admitted that his given name, Maximilian, had caused him a few uncomfortable moments during his lifetime.

They both fell to wondering what prompted parents to endow their offspring with such outlandish names. He had been named Max after his father, who, in turn, had gotten the appellation from his father. Buffy didn't know, of course, if she had inherited Bernadine from some poor unfortunate relative who also had that name. However, she did say it was a crime that these kinds of names got passed down from generation to generation. Max agreed, but then admitted quite blandly, with tongue in cheek, that he had every intention of naming his first son Max.

It was a pleasant yet exciting morning. As if by silent mutual consent, no mention was made of Jeffrey Dunstan or Buffy's engagement to him. It was as if he didn't exist, as he might as well not have for all the thought she gave to him. She actually couldn't dredge up a very clear picture of him in her mind, her sight being so full of the incredible Max Shepherd.

Before pulling into the boat dock Max motored her around the periphery of the island. She noticed a large black hole in some rock on the north side of the island. He explained that it was a cave, and under no circumstances was she to ever go anywhere near it, for the waters breaking upon it were treacherous.

After lunch they sat on the side of Ponsonby's pool for a while, talking quietly. It was Max who brought up the subject of tennis.

"What are you going to do this afternoon?" he asked.

"Sleep," she answered, stifling a yawn.

"How about a set of tennis after your nap?" he asked.

He was setting himself up beautifully. She slipped into the bright aquamarine pool water and submerged her golden body for a while, moving with lazy, scissorlike kicks. At length she surfaced and shook her wildly curly head.

Trying not to laugh, she warned, "I'm very good, Max."

"I'm well aware of that. I've been watching your career for quite sometime now."

"Really?" Her arms made lazy movements at her sides as she tried to absorb this bit of news. She found it difficult to believe that he had been avidly reading about her successes in the sports section of the *Miami Times*, the paper which seemed to consider her their own special darling.

"Yes. I even saw you play a couple of times before you came to Palm Isle for our tournament."

"When?" she queried.

"Last spring in Atlantic City, then again in Lauderdale. It just happened that my business took me to those places during the times of the tournaments."

"I can't imagine a big resort owner like yourself going to tennis tournaments in his spare time," she scoffed.

"Let's just say that I have an interest in the sport, which goes way back."

"Okay, Max." She grinned impishly. "I'd love to play

68

you." She did a backward somersault to keep from laughing in his face.

"You'll go easy on the old man, won't you?" he asked as she came up.

She floated over to him again, taking in his muscular, athletic body, his handsome, angular face, and his silver-sheened eyes, which held a secret smile.

"Oh, yes," she promised solemnly, having no intentions of doing so.

He held out a hand and helped her nubile, bikini-clad body to the deck. "Go on, then," he said. "Have your nap. I'll meet you on the court at fiveish. That will give us plenty of time for a good rousing set before dinner."

She nodded agreeably and padded off to the private door to her room, the promise of certain victory tasting marvelously sweet in her mischievously smiling mouth.

Once in her room, she showered, washed her hair, and settled down for a restful nap, wondering before dropping off if she should really mutilate him on the court. After all, he was, sometimes, incredibly nice.

Buffy woke at four-thirty and groomed herself as carefully as if she were going to a tournament. While donning a yellow sport dress the color of lemon sunshine, she wondered again how badly she should beat him. Just bringing him to his knees should suffice. It wouldn't be sporting to totally obliterate him. On the other hand, total obliteration would give her such a sense of power. Yes, she decided, this wasn't a time to be squeamish; it had to be quick and absolute annihilation.

She grabbed up her tennis racket and a clean hand towel and headed for the court. The die was cast. She crossed the pine grove that divided the court from the house with much the same grim determination as Caesar when he crossed the Rubicon.

Dressed in tennis whites, Max was sitting in a chair at an umbrellaed table by the courts, waiting. He got to his feet immediately at her appearance.

"You're looking incredibly beautiful. I can't remember ever playing anyone so lovely."

She gave him a sweet, almost shy, smile as her wicked resolution wavered for an instant. He was so gallant, so much the gentleman, with his grandiose flattery.

She won the first serve and soon had him moving from one side of the court to the other. He returned her balls with precise popping sounds. This both piqued and puzzled her. He had every bit as much assurance on the court as he had everywhere else. At length he sent her a smasher with a top spin that she missed.

"Lucky break," she muttered, raking sweat from her brow. She grew more aggressive. But to her amazement, he did, too.

After over an hour of hard, steady playing, she had won five games. But he had won six! She was in a swelter of angry confusion. How had he done it? Somehow he had managed to always be in the right place at the right time. And those wicked slicing spins he put on the ball made her head throb.

She walked to the net and bent to untie and retie her shoelaces—a standard signal among tennis players that a breather was necessary. When she looked up, she saw him towering over her, his arms hanging negligently over the net as he flashed her a self-possessed, lazy white grin.

Sudden, uncontrollable anger coursed through her like a bolt of lightning, causing her to tremble from the force of it.

"I'm going to smear you," she threatened, totally losing her cool.

"Ah, Buffy," he chortled, "you are both a delight and a challenge."

She viciously grabbed her racket and a ball and positioned herself behind the serving line. This last crucial game was fought with silent, grim intensity. Due to the black, smoldering anger that gripped her, she made some errors in judgment and fell behind.

She realized that he had already defeated her psychologically—certain death in any game. Heroically, in spite of her blinding resentment, she pulled herself together sufficiently to even the score. They fought over the game point

70

for nearly twenty minutes. Finally he put a neat undercut on the ball, causing it to spin rakishly off to one side after bouncing at her feet. She swung at it crazily, missing it by a mile and making herself look quite ridiculous.

She heard his loud laughter but saw nothing as she turned in a blind rage and threw the finest racket Wilson ever made to the hard surface of the court, snapping it in two at the neck.

Then she whirled toward his approaching white figure, which had just bounded over the net, and favored him with every vile curse she had ever learned since leaving the orphanage, which was a considerable amount.

He picked her up like a piece of baggage, walked resolutely to the chair by the gay floral umbrella, forced her enraged, kicking body over his knee, and administered a sound spanking to her bright-yellow backside.

When he released her, she jumped to her feet, holding trembling hands to her stinging derriere. Tears of hurt and humiliation streamed down her face. She felt completely devastated in body and soul.

"Oh, I hate you, I hate you!" she sobbed before turning and running to her room.

She cried violently into her purple velvet bedspread, luxuriating in the hard physical sobs which racked her.

At length Max came in and sat down beside her. She turned away from him awkwardly, snuffling convulsively.

"I brought you some tea."

"Go away," she cried, wiping tears from her cheeks with splayed, shaking fingers.

"I'm sorry I had to do that." He put his hand on her shoulder, and she lunged away.

"Leave me alone."

"I can't, sweet girl."

She stole a glance at him and saw a strange look of anguish on his face, which she didn't understand.

"Come along, now." He smiled. "Have a cup of Ponsonby's famous English tea. It will make you feel better."

She sat up slowly and took the tea. "How did you beat me?" she asked incredulously as she sniffed piteously over

71

the cup. Her curiosity about his expertise overrode every other consideration, even the utter degradation of being spanked by him.

He reached out and brushed a curl away from her hot, perspiring forehead. "You let me rattle you. You could have beat me perhaps, if you had kept your composure."

"Perhaps?"

"Yes. You need to learn more technique, Buffy. You've been poorly coached."

She sipped her tea and allowed its aromatic flavor to soothe her. "How do you know so much about it?" she asked quietly.

"Along about the time you first began to wield a tennis racket, I was winning at Wimbledon," he confessed.

She choked over her teacup and quickly set it aside. "You won at Wimbledon! When?"

"Ten years ago, when I was twenty-three. I decided not to go on with my career in tennis because Dad needed me so badly in the business. But I still play every chance I get. I came up against some of the best during a trip to Australia last month."

She sat before him, a heap of golden bewilderment. "I had no idea."

"I know. I'm afraid I set you up for that out there." He nodded in the direction of the court. "But it wasn't because I wanted to hurt you in any way. I just wanted to play you and perhaps give you a few pointers I've learned along the way. You have great promise," he declared, giving her a broad smile. "You'll make it to Wimbledon someday."

"Do you really think so?"

"It is inevitable," he stated. "But you do need to learn a few things. You're gutty. But it takes more than guts to win at Wimbledon; it takes some finesse."

"Can you teach me that fantastic back undercut you used against me today?" she asked him eagerly.

"That, and more," he promised, "if you'll let me."

She inched closer to him and mumbled shyly, "I'll let you."

"No more temper tantrums, then," he whispered softly.

"I'm sorry. I didn't mean those horrible things I said to you. I won't do it again."

"I didn't want to hurt you—to make you cry."

She looked down at his hand, which was clenched into the bedcovers. It was a strong hand, deeply sinewed with dark, short hairs softly curling across it and around an expensive gold watch on his wrist.

"I didn't hurt you badly, did I?" he asked, seeming to crave a kind of reassurance from her.

"Well, you sure didn't tickle me," she informed him stoutly.

He laughed then, a resounding laugh, which vibrated his chest and the air that surrounded them. Then he hugged her, and she laughed, too.

"Friends?" he asked, kissing the top of her head.

"Friends," she agreed, wondering whether Max had been created on earth or in heaven.

As she prepared for dinner that evening, she tried honestly and with a sort of groping desperation to come to terms with her relationship with this strange and exciting man named Max Shepherd.

They had called a truce. She was glad of that, because battling with Max was definitely beyond her scope. But what did he think of her? Obviously he cared for her a little, or he wouldn't spend so much time in her company; neither would he volunteer to teach her his hard-earned tennis techniques. Yet she feared he regarded her in somewhat the same manner as the two boys he looked out after on Nassau. Like them, she challenged his protective instincts. He was a substitute father to them; an older brother to her. Suddenly she sighed deeply, feeling inexplicably sad. A kid sister—that was all she was to him.

She decided to boost her morale by dressing up for dinner. She put on the fanciest of the two dresses she had brought. It was a pink full chiffon, which cinched her tiny waist and came off her sloping, youthful shoulders in a wide feminine ruffle.

After she was fully dressed and groomed she critically

examined herself in the mirror, then grimaced. She looked like Shirley Temple on her way to the *Good Ship Lollipop*. Max would go for the highly sophisticated type. Buffy pictured a tall, dark, serpentine creature slinking along in black satin, a cocktail glass tinkling musically in one hand.

She pulled the bodice of the dress down to the white lace of her strapless bra and turned this way and that. A definite, but hardly voluptuous, cleavage presented itself. Patting the dress back into place, she shook her head. What was she thinking of? Max would never see her as anything other than a naughty child. Besides, she was still engaged to Jeffrey. She must remember that, even though she was unaccountably relieved, now that she had not been able to show up for their wedding.

Dinner was not quite ready, so she joined Max in the living room, where he was taking a before-dinner drink.

"Charming." He raised his glass as a toast to her appearance. "May I fix you a drink?"

"No, thanks." She sat down on the lush white couch and looked dreamily out wide windows at a moonlit, shimmering sea.

He sat beside her and scrutinized her profile, his keen eyes becoming dark with the turbulence of his thoughts. "You possess all the fresh innocence of a lovely rose before coming into full bloom. It's quite rare these days."

"What are you talking about?" she asked warily.

"Virginity." He toasted her again. "It envelopes you like a fragrance."

A deep roseate flush crept across her bare shoulders and into her smooth, flawless cheeks. "I was raised in a religious environment. Strange as it may seem," she explained in an uncomfortable voice, "I have morals."

"Please don't apologize." A wry smile raised one side of his sensuous, well-cut mouth.

"Besides," she went on, "tennis takes up all my time and devotion. Getting myself into affairs that lead nowhere would be distracting."

"Do you ever dream of Dunstan making love to you?"

74

he asked with devastating suddenness.

"Max!" She was shocked.

"I'm sorry," he apologized, looking into his drink. "I had no right to ask that."

"N-no," she protested haltingly. "It's all right, really." She wanted desperately to be honest with him, and with herself. "I've thought of it, naturally," she admitted. "Jeffrey and I were planning to be married. But I can't honestly say I dreamed of it night and day." She shrugged, unable to express her doubts and uncertainties concerning the subject.

"Do you really know what love is at all, my sweet?"

"Probably not," she admitted. "I have never witnessed it first hand; nor have I ever been truly loved, parentally or otherwise." It cost her a great deal to say this, but she was becoming increasingly aware that what was between herself and Jeffrey was not the deep, abiding love one goes through life longing for. "As I told you before, all-consuming love seems an unrealistic element to me. It belongs to a world I've never been a part of."

"Would you recognize it if you met it head-on?" he quizzed.

"Do I look stupid?" she snapped.

"No." He laughed soundlessly. "But I'm beginning to believe you are—frightfully so."

"Dinner, sir," announced Loa from the dining room doorway.

"Come along." He rose gracefully from the couch, extending a hand and pulling her up to his side. "Allow me to enjoy a lovely dinner with a lovely . . . woman."

And Buffy couldn't help but notice how he had stumbled over the word "woman."

CHAPTER 5

For the next couple of days Buffy and Max were on the court every morning before the sun got hot. Since she had broken her beloved racket, she made use of one of Ponsonby's, several of which he kept handy in the utility room. Max taught her new techniques, and she was quick to learn. Then, in the evenings before dinner, they were again on the courts, Buffy eager to learn all she could in the shortest possible time.

Jeffrey and her job at Waterbrook seemed to belong to another world, a world that wasn't relative to her. She put off thinking about her departure from Ponsonby's Paradise, for it meant separation from Max. That they would eventually go their separate ways seemed a malicious trick of fate, for Max, in less than a week, had become an integral part of her life. She was loathe to even let him out of her sight.

One morning she woke early, anticipating another day in his company. She dressed quickly in her tennis togs and walked through the silent hall to the even more silent kitchen; Loa had not arrived yet. She put coffee on, then while it perked she ambled idly out to the mist-swathed pool area.

Suddenly she froze in terror. Draped across the deck was a large brown horny crocodile, which blinked at her somnambulantly.

She squeaked, shook her head in disbelief, closed her eyes, then opened them again. Yes, it was really a crocodile. As she began to inch backward the huge reptile came alive. He rose up on all fours and waddled toward her lazily, opening his cottony mouth to bare an impressive array of deadly fangs.

"N-nice b-boy." She held up a halting hand as she continued to wobble backward, stumbling into chairs and tables in the process.

He came to a halt not three feet from her and uttered a loud hiss from his open maw. She gasped, turned, and scrambled through the glass doors, closing them spastically.

"Maaaax," she screamed like a siren, running in panic to his room, bursting through his door, and landing square in the middle of his bed.

Silky dark hair atousle, he turned from his comfortable position and regarded her with mingled confusion and concern. "What the devil is wrong with you this morning?"

She gulped, raised her hands to her curly head, and whispered, "You won't believe it!" She swallowed thickly and went on. "There's a big, nasty crocodile out by the pool. He nearly took my leg off."

Max put a tanned bare arm behind his head and regarded her with amusement.

"I'm not kidding!" she screeched. "Get up!" She pulled at his covers, but he held them tenaciously. It was then that an obvious fact dawned upon her addled brain—Max had nothing on. He was one of those men who slept in the raw.

"Wait for me outside the door," he instructed her. "I'll be out directly to make acquaintance with this beast of yours."

"You don't believe me," she flashed.

"Of course I believe you," he assured her evenly.

"Oh, how can you be so calm all the time?" she fumed as she hurried to the door. "It's positively inhuman."

He joined her in less than two minutes outside the door, wearing only a pair of white tennis shorts. He stopped in the kitchen, poured a cup of coffee, and took a couple of quick sips. Then he opened the refrigerator door and rummaged around inside.

"This is no time for breakfast!" she expostulated as she ran to the glass doors fearfully. She had no trouble spotting the monster: he was in the same threatening stance in which she had left him.

"Ah, yes." Max came up behind her. "He is quite large, isn't he?"

Max opened the glass door and, to Buffy's utter amazement, threw a raw frankfurter into the animal's brightly moist, cavernous mouth. The creature bit down in slow motion, blinked sleepily, then lumbered off, his fat, unattractive tail swinging nightmarishly behind.

Buffy uttered a sigh of pure relief and rested the back of her head against the window.

"That was Ponsonby's pet crocodile, Sigmund," Max informed her laughingly. "He usually roosts up in the cliffs on the north side of the island by a fresh spring. Apparently there's an underground river flowing beneath the island, which surfaces into a fresh pool on the cliff where you saw the cave the other day. There is a lot of lush greenery there, and that is where Sigmund makes his abode. Some mischievous friend gave him to Pons years ago when he was just a cute little reptile. Pons kept him, realizing in him a constant source of entertainment where unsuspecting guests are concerned."

"This Lord Ponsonby must be the worst kind of eccentric," she observed weakly.

"Pons does love a good practical joke," he admitted ruefully. "He claims it's the unexpected that makes for comedy in life."

"Well, I didn't think Sigmund was very funny." She took a deep, steadying breath.

He took her hand and bowed over it mockingly. "I feel so very brave. I've slain my first dragon. And saved the lady fair."

"Oh, you're impossible," she said exasperatedly. "If I'd have known all the ugly thing wanted was a hot dog, I'd have thrown it at him myself." Then mellowing in the aftermath of her panic, she commented generously, "Poor

79

thing. He's probably terribly lonely all by himself up there on that cliff."

"Yes," Max agreed solemnly, "I imagine he's quite horny, indeed."

"Oh, you're awful!" She slapped at him and stalked into the kitchen.

They talked and joked as they prepared breakfast together. After eating, Max relaxed back in his chair and lit a cheroot, while Buffy fidgeted about in the kitchen restlessly.

"Do you realize that it's been six days since we've seen a newspaper?" she asked.

"So what?" His firm lips made an O as he blew a cloud of smoke toward the ceiling. "We can listen to the news on the radio."

"It's just that I always pore over the paper after breakfast. It's a habit."

"What a beastly way to begin the day." He continued to puff with obvious pleasure. "What part of the paper do you read?" He gave her a look which, to her mind, indicated he didn't think her intellect capable of much more than the comics and the sports section.

"All of it," she averred stoutly. "When I have time I even tackle the crossword puzzle."

"Ah, yes, the crossword puzzle." He smoked on blithely. "The best sort of method to learn difficult, yet useless, words. Give me a three-letter word for an African antelope," he demanded.

"Gnu," she responded quickly.

"A five letter word meaning to expunge?"

"Erase," she responded smugly. "That was too easy."

"A passionate affection for someone of the opposite sex—a four-letter word."

"Love," she whispered, sitting down at the table, her legs suddenly feeling shaky. "Another easy one."

"Really?" He stubbed out his cigar and pierced her with his keen, assessing, gray gaze. "I would have thought you'd only recognize that word in its relation to tennis. It means

80

zero in tennis and apparently adds up to the same in your life."

"It's not my fault I've never been in love," she explained irritably. "No one has ever really shown me what it's all about. No one has ever really loved me."

"Not even Dunstan?" he posed quietly.

Buffy sighed defeatedly and admitted, "Not even Jeffrey. He feels something for me, I know. But it's not love."

"Well, well, we're making progress." He leaned back in his chair, gloating.

She shifted uncomfortably and groped to change the subject. "I suppose you only read the financial page of the paper?" she asked.

"That and the sports section. I also do crossword puzzles occasionally to unwind my mind." He leaned over his empty plate toward her and taunted, "So you see, we have a great deal in common—yogurt, crossword puzzles, tennis."

He was making a joke, pretending they were compatible when really they were worlds apart. She looked at him, a sudden undefinable longing darkening her honey-gold eyes as an incredible hurting need suffused her, leaving her lonely and sad.

When they were out on the courts, Max spent the morning trying to perfect Buffy's backhand. He held her from behind as if they were one person, explicitly demonstrating the angle of the swing. For the first time in her life, she found it impossible to concentrate on the game.

He worked with her patiently, but finally concluded that she was just having a bad day and suggested they go down on the beach for a while before lunch.

They changed and headed for the beach. Sharing the same towel, they lay side by side on their stomachs. Max watched as a warm breeze lifted her curls, then let them down again gently. He closed his eyes to blot out the delicate gold of her, the exquisitely parted lips.

Assuming he had fallen asleep, she stared at him intently. So this was British nobility: dark aristocratic head;

broad forehead; straight, well-formed nose; firm cleft chin, which hinted of both strength and stubbornness; a full, wide, disturbingly sensuous mouth.

Desire, which lay in the depths of her midsection like a sleeping kitten, roused and stretched itself in one writhing motion, nearly shattering her with unfamiliar sensations.

"You're bothering me," he muttered irritably. "I'm trying to sleep."

"I'm not doing a thing," she protested with a breathless gasp.

"Go play in the surf or something," he suggested, turning his head, settling it back down into the towel with a sigh.

She continued to lay beside him, not touching him, yet all too aware of their closeness. Dark wet hairs curled on his perspiring neck; sweat glossed his thick, wide shoulders. One of his hands twitched slightly, and she gathered he had slipped into a doze.

She got up quietly, as if putting some distance between them was absolutely imperative, and perched herself gaminely on a large piece of driftwood. From that angle she continued to examine him as if mesmerized. He was perfect. No man had a right to be so godlike.

Her gaze rested on his bare legs, and she smiled inwardly. She began to hum tunelessly with satisfaction.

He stirred irritably. "I warn you," he said, barely audibly. "I am quite a tiger when awakened."

She chuckled, picked up a handful of broken shells, and began to pelt his legs with them one at a time.

"What the devil are you doing?" he grunted, still refusing to move.

"Practicing my aim." A shell hit his hard, darkly haired calf and bounced off. "Bull's-eye!"

"You are a wicked child."

"I hate to tell you this, Max," she taunted. "I'm sure it will be a terrible blow to your ego. But I've found a flaw in you."

"I'm warning you, Buffy." He was fully conscious now, but still prostrate.

"Well, don't you want to know what it is?"

"No."

"You're slightly bowlegged, Max." She delivered this information as if he possessed some freakish disfigurement.

"That does it." He was up now, lunging for her gracelessly. She shrieked and ran to the water's edge, where he overtook her, picking her up bodily and slinging her into the surf, arms and legs awry.

Then he followed her in, and they played like a couple of crazy children, laughing, grabbing, ducking, and rolling in the water together.

At what point this childish madness evolved into something poignantly adult, Buffy didn't know. She only knew that a wave had washed them ashore, their arms and legs were entangled, and Max was on top of her.

The sun stood in awe; the world went silent. His head bent toward her as if drawn by a force stronger than magic. She waited for what seemed like an eternity, longing to taste the salt on his lips and the masculine sweetness beyond.

"God!" he gasped, close to her mouth. "What am I doing?" All at once he was up, pulling her to her feet. "Get up," he ordered gruffly, "before I forget every noble promise I made to myself about you."

She stood before him, feeling like a piece of unsubstantial flotsam.

"It must be about lunchtime," he said matter-of-factly as he walked over to pick up their towel. "Loa will be expecting us."

Just like Max to calmly speak of lunch when her whole world had been about to explode into blinding, kaleidoscopic passion. The precious moment between them had meant nothing to him.

"Yes." She pulled herself together stalwartly. "Let's not forget about lunch."

Myaka was in the kitchen with Loa when they entered. He grinned at them, revealing nearly every pearly-white tooth in his head; Loa looked like the cat who had just swallowed the proverbial canary.

83

What's up? Buffy wondered. Why are they acting so strangely?

Max was silent through lunch and Buffy sensed that he had withdrawn from her in some inexplicable way. It had been abundantly clear that he hadn't wanted to kiss her; which was why he didn't when the opportunity had so unexpectedly presented itself.

He got up immediately after lunch, laying his napkin on the glass top of the table with deliberate calm. "Myaka and I are going to change the oil in the plane this afternoon," he announced, bowing distantly and exiting with haste.

A slap couldn't have hurt her more. She and Max had been practically inseparable in the six days they had known one another. Now he was showing all too plainly that he wanted to get away from her. Perhaps he and Myaka had actually made a date to work on the plane. Nevertheless, his obvious desire to grasp at this as an excuse to get away hurt Buffy terribly.

She went to her room and changed into shorts, wearing with them a white halter top that was held up by only a thin band of elastic and the provocative swell of her young breasts.

She tried to swallow a lump that refused to dislodge itself from her throat as she surmised that Max had finally grown tired of her. Having someone he considered an immature kid around all the time was a bother to him.

How she longed to be a really stunning woman—a sleek, self-assured sophisticate who could make Max turn flips of ardor; a dark, lithe, long-legged woman who could give him one look through darkly fringed lids and turn him into a ravening animal bent on lust.

She sat down on the bed and laughed weakly at her own foolish imaginings. Dreams—merely dreams. And where could dreams, or the brief fulfillment of them, for that matter, get her when separation from him in the short space of one week was inevitable.

She'd better pull herself together where Max Shepherd was concerned. He was inaccessible.

She briefly entertained the idea of trying to seduce him by acting flirtatious, but discarded this notion the very instant it whizzed through her brain. She was not the least bit sexy and didn't know how to begin feigning it at this late date. She couldn't tempt Max no matter what alluring tricks she tried to pull out of a magic hat. She could only be Buffy—and that was sadly inadequate.

Besides, mad affairs were totally foreign to her. That sort of thing was not a part of her life-style. A brief fling with Max here in Ponsonby's Paradise would be earth-shaking, to say the least, but it would devastate her self-respect. She had responsibilities to Jeffrey; to her profession; to dear, gentle Mr. J., who had tried so hard to raise her properly; and to herself.

Oh, well, the whole question was academic: Max wouldn't be interested anyway. Unless perhaps at gunpoint. She giggled and with unconscious youthful grace bounced on silent sneakers into the kitchen.

Loa beamed a Cheshire cat grin at her, and Buffy again had the distinct impression that something was afoot.

"Okay, Loa, spill it," she demanded, snitching an apple from a nearby fruit bowl and biting into it noisily.

"Spill it?" the servant asked uncomprehendingly, apparently not familiar with this idiom.

"Yes. Tell me what's going on."

"You should know." Loa sidled her a sly glance.

Buffy hoisted her boyishly slender derriere to the mandarine-orange kitchen counter. "Yes. I should know a lot of things." She bit into her apple morosely. "I thought I did know a lot of things. Until I met Max." She tossed the half-eaten apple into the trash and tucked her knee under her chin. "I think I must be somewhere betwixt and between," she mumbled inaudibly.

Loa clicked her tongue and rolled her eyes happily. "You and Mr. Shepherd make a fine couple. Me and my man, we been wanting to see Mr. Shepherd get him a woman for a long time. We are so glad for you both."

"What, for heaven's sake, are you talking about?"

"My man see you and Mr. Shepherd kissing on the beach."

Buffy groaned. All she needed now was this ebony cupid and her husband jumping to erroneous conclusions. "We weren't kissing. We almost did, but . . . but it didn't work out . . ." her voice trailed off, "or something."

"But he will make love to you soon," Loa stated unperturbedly. "He wants you."

"Oh, Loa, you're wrong." She jumped down from the counter and flopped into a nearby chair. "Max would never go for me." She waved her hand and laughed hollowly. "The Peter Pan of Ponsonby's Paradise!"

"My man say you are just what young Mr. Shepherd has looked for all these years." Loa pursed her lips firmly. "My man, he never wrong. He say you are as fresh as a sunbeam. You make Mr. Shepherd laugh. You bring him happiness. And Mr. Shepherd make you happy when you lie in his arms."

Buffy let out a shocked gasp and wiggled in her seat as if it were full of hot tacks.

"Now I embarr . . . embarra . . ."

"Embarrass," Buffy supplied.

"Yes. Embarrass you."

"Maybe. A little," Buffy admitted. "But only because you are so mistaken. Max treats me like a kid sister. Haven't you noticed?"

"I see Mr. Shepherd follow you with his eyes. He hunger for you. I know these things," the servant put in stoutly. "And when a man like that make you his woman, it is like . . ." She glanced about the gleaming kitchen, searching for words.

"Like what?" Buffy quizzed, her curiosity overriding the whole ridiculous argument. "What's it like, Loa?"

"Like an angel has spread his wings over you. Earth and heaven, they are one. Your man, he take you into his soul. And you ride in the sky together. It can only happen between those who truly love. I know."

Buffy closed her eyes. To know! What bliss! How lucky

86

Loa was. For all her simplistic outlook on life, she had plumbed a woman's deepest secrets.

"I make you and Mr. Shepherd a good meal tonight. I leave early. Then you and Mr. Shepherd—"

"Now hold on a minute," Buffy halted her. She couldn't allow Loa to go on with this wild fantasy and even wilder plotting. "Max and I are of two different worlds. There's absolutely no chance of our ever getting together."

But Loa merely smiled knowingly. "It will happen. No matter if you are millions of worlds apart, you will come together as the wave kisses the sand. It is right. You belong to one another, even now." She set herself to scrubbing some potatoes in the sink, adding mildly, "That Marlene, she think she got Mr. Shepherd. She get fooled pretty damn good."

It was as if a bomb had exploded somewhere in the vicinity of Buffy's brain. "And who, pray tell, is Marlene?"

"Boss's daughter." Loa attacked a potato without mercy, and Buffy gathered that the servant felt pretty strongly about Marlene.

"And this Marlene," Buffy quizzed. "She is sort of Max's girl friend?"

"She everybody's woman." Loa blew out a scornful, noisy breath. "Mr. Shepherd, he don't love her, he love you."

Buffy looked up to heaven, as she couldn't believe this servant's persistent hanging on to such a mad illusion. Finally she stretched her slim, petite legs, got up, and walked over to Loa, putting her arm around her.

"You're a fruitcake," she accused the velvety black face that smiled back at her. Loa nodded in agreement and Buffy laughed, realizing then that Loa had never heard this slang term. "I like you."

"I like you too, Miss Buffy."

"I'm going off to explore the island," she announced, heading for the door. "I haven't thoroughly been over it yet."

"You stay away from that cave in the north side," Loa ordered in no uncertain terms. "The water there is bad."

"Okay." Buffy waved unconcernedly as she hurried out the door.

She walked down the shaded road from Ponsonby's Palace with long, even strides. Her shoes didn't make a sound as they came down on the heavy blanket of pine straw that lay over the road. Her arms moved rhythmically at her sides and her skin and hair felt washed with the clean and lively air of Ponsonby's Paradise.

When she reached the bottom of the hill, she paused for a while, considering whether or not she should go down to the airstrip to let Max know her plans.

As she stood biting her lip irresolutely a revelation dawned upon her: She missed Max. It was less than an hour since she'd last seen him—and she missed him dreadfully. She longed to see him, to hear his masculine voice and that deep, lazy laughter.

She moved to take the path to the airfield. It would be only common courtesy to drop by and tell him where she was going. Perhaps she would even hang around a while and watch him work.

She brought herself up short. Who was she trying to fool? She wanted to be with Max more than anything else in the world. And he certainly didn't feel the same way. He'd made that only too plain at lunch. She hoped she had a little more pride than to tag after a guy like a little puppy. Besides, hadn't Loa intimated that Max was in pretty deep with Ponsonby's daughter, Marlene? The idea of chasing after a man repelled her. And chasing after one who was involved with someone else repelled her to the point of near nausea.

She shook herself irritably and turned deliberately off the path to the airstrip. She walked, instead, toward the beach. What she felt for Max was infatuation, she told herself with a knowing smile. What woman could keep from falling for him a little bit? She was attracted to his charm, to his blatant, yet controlled, maleness. Any woman would be.

Once she was back in Miami with Jeffrey she would wonder how she had ever become so enthralled by Max.

88

Right now she was merely under a strange spell because of being on this beautiful island virtually alone with him.

Approaching the ever undulating sea, she made an abrupt turn and walked along the firm damp sand at the high-tide line. Breaking into a gentle jog, she continued to think. It was not possible to fall in love with a man in less than a week. Such things only happen in movies.

She recalled seeing the movie version of *Romeo and Juliet* when she was a young teen-ager. At a dance Romeo had looked at Juliet; Juliet had looked at Romeo; music had crescendoed; love had burst into full bloom. Then he was scaling the castle wall at night to get to her room.

Love at first sight—it was too glib, too unbelievable. But she remembered that heart-stopping moment on the steps of Palm Isle Resort when she had bent to tie her shoe and looked up to find Max's disturbing gray eyes upon her. But that wasn't love at first sight, she reasoned. That was just some kind of unusual man-woman awareness.

Yes, she did have a woman's awareness of Max. She had to admit that. Every time he touched her she warmed. And when she had lain with him on the beach this morning, a pulsating desire had whipped through her. Then, in the surf, she had longed for his kiss to the extent that all she could imagine was the feel of him; the manly, fragrant taste of him. Oh, it was all so ridiculous. She was engaged to Jeffrey, and Max was probably having some sort of running affair with this Marlene.

Buffy was jogging toward the lagoon now, beyond which Myaka and Loa's house was located. She was certain she wasn't in love with Max. Everything she felt for him added up to infatuation—nothing more. How futile it would be to really fall in love with a man like that under the circumstances.

She stepped up her pace and lunged at the hill upon which the servants' house rested, taking it with great bone-breaking strides. Panting for breath and her heart near to bursting, she reached the top and threw herself facedown in tall, wheat-colored grass. She wanted desperately to burst into tears, but wouldn't give into it. She lay her cheek against the warm grass and breathed evenly until her pulses quietened, saying over and over to herself, I haven't fallen in love with Max Shepherd, I couldn't be that stupid. It's infatuation, merely infatuation.

Finally she rose from the grass and walked slowly toward the garden that lay in back of the servant's bungalow-style house. Here she found a large, well-kept plot of growing vegetables. There were turnips, peas, tomatoes, lettuce, broccoli, squash, and other vegetables that she did not readily recognize.

She realized this would be the second garden of the year, since tropical climates enjoy two growing seasons. Indeed, it was possible to keep some kind of vegetable growing all year round in Florida. She had seen black-eyed peas and eggplant growing in Mrs. Johnson's garden in August. She had also seen broccoli and greens thriving all through a Florida winter. But tomatoes never made it into the coolest winter months, their pungent and delicate vines being too susceptible to cold.

Buffy walked over to the row of tomato vines. Myaka had tied each vine in several places to a stake. Some of the tomatoes were large beefsteaks, turning pink in the hot sun; others were small salad tomatoes about the size of cherries. She picked one of these, a very plump red one, and tossed it into her mouth. It was warm and burst deliciously in her mouth as she bit into it.

Beyond the garden lay a grove of citrus trees. None of the fruit was ripe yet. She could tell grapefruit from oranges, but could not distinguish the many different types of orange trees that were growing in the grove. She did, however, recognize a tangerine tree by its ridged fruit, now green and about the size of large mushroom heads.

Buffy went on beyond the grove to admire a large stand of banana trees and some guava bushes. She was sorry that the guavas were past bearing, for she loved the smell of the fruit even though she found the taste a little too strong. This explained the lovely homemade guava jelly she and Max enjoyed on their toast every morning.

Loa must be kept terribly busy from early spring to

deep summer, canning and freezing fruits and vegetables. Then in the fall she would probably have to do greens and tomatoes. By the looks of the tomato vines, she would have her work cut out for her this season. And with this climate, even more tropical than that of Florida, there must be a veritable abundance of things that would grow right on through the winter. Certainly the citrus would ripen to its full golden lusciousness in the cool of the winter. Loa would then spend her time juicing and sectioning fruit for the freezer.

Buffy realized now that the melon and oranges she had been enjoying with her yogurt at lunch each day, instead of being fresh, had been frozen. She had noticed it being a bit different in texture, but it was so delicious, she hardly thought to question it.

In a little open clearing she discovered Ponsonby's source of fresh eggs. A neat white chicken coop stood under an orange tree, the whole thing—coop, tree, and surrounding circle—being enclosed by chicken wire. Fluffy proud hens were roosting in the foliage of the tree while others pecked after bugs on the ground. A magnificent colorful rooster strutted the territory, keeping his harem quite under control.

Buffy laughed and skirted around the coop, heading back down the hill toward the beach. She was walking toward the north side of the island now, where the cave was. She could see the cliff of black rock that housed it, jutting out to sea like an angry forehead.

There was a barrier of black rock that ranged out to sea, making a sort of interesting jetty. Buffy wondered if she dared walk out on these rocks and take a peek at the cave; it would certainly be visible from the farthest point of the jetty.

Max had warned her not to go near the cave. Loa too had said that the waters were dangerous. But walking out on solid rock so that she could look back into the cave would not be risky at all, she reasoned.

She began to step gingerly on the rocks, surefooted and confident. Some of them were slippery, but she made very sure of them before putting her full weight down. The jetty was about three feet wide, and the waves splashing up against the rocks on her left side occasionally doused her legs and sneakers.

She walked like a tightrope artist, glancing to her left frequently. So far she saw nothing that would indicate that the waters that lay in the vicinity of the cave were overly treacherous. Waves were pounding against the rocks, but that was normal, for the tide was beginning to come in.

Feeling quite safe as she traversed the last couple of yards of the jetty, she did not closely examine the nature of the water, so sure was she that it was merely normal high tide water full of gentle, deep swells, which would overwhelm a beginning swimmer certainly, but not her.

At last reaching the remotest large rock of the line, she stood up, one hand shading her eyes, and looked back toward the cave. It was too black to see inside, but she could see that the bottom of it was flooded with water, a swift water that worked contrary to the incoming tide. She remembered Max telling her that the cliff above the cave had a fresh spring. Perhaps the same river that fed it also coursed its way through this cave, gushing into the sea with great force.

She looked closely at the water in front of the cave and then immediately in front of her. What she saw turned her blood to ice. The water was rolling and writhing as if it contained a million frenzied snakes.

Like a victim of Medusa, she seemed to turn to stone. If a person were caught in that water, it would mean the end. The various conflicting currents would drag one under into their boiling bowels until one's breath turned to water. Later, perhaps, the sea would mercifully spit up its victim onto a sugar-white beach to be found by a loved one.

"Buffy!" came a distant yell from the beach.

She turned and saw Max standing some distance down the beach, waving at her frantically.

"Max!" she gulped, in a pitiful plea. "Oh, Max!"

Suddenly it was the most important thing in her life to get off that jetty and into Max's arms.

He started to run down the beach toward her, and she began groping over the rocks toward him. But after not taking more than three steps, she slipped and tumbled, almost in slow motion, into the dangerously active water.

She didn't even scream, just raised her helpless hand toward Max as she went under. Her knees scraped some rock as the swift current carried her out in soft, suffocating rolls.

She beat the water with her arms and legs, trying to find air. But all sense of direction had been obliterated. She was in the worst of the mad, tearing current now. She didn't know what was up, or what was down. Daylight appeared for a brief instant. She gulped it into her bursting lungs and tried to hold some of it in her fist. But a green wall of water toppled over her and bore her down again.

She opened her mouth again for air and swallowed water. All resistence left her limbs as they wilted into rubbery slackness. Blackness moved in to displace all that green. She said to herself in awe before completely losing consciousness, "Why, I'm going to die."

Time must have passed, for when daylight swam before her again, her back was against hard sand. Everything was vague, but breath was being forced into her lungs. It was Max. She accepted his oxygen, coughed, gasped, and began to breath on her own.

A wave of nausea passed over her and she turned away from him to quietly spew seawater into the sand. Then she remained motionless for a while still, dizzy and sick—and embarrassed that she had done such an unglamorous thing in front of Max.

"You'll be all right," he said weakly from behind her. He turned her over to face him, and she realized with shock what he must have gone through to save her life. He was totally exhausted.

"Thank you, Max," she whimpered.

He drew her into his arms. She felt his solid wall of a

chest, and the whole length of his body became an anchor to her. She snuggled into him and wanted to go right on into the very essence of his being. It was as if all her life she'd been waiting for him. He was a shelter, a safe place, a rock to cling to in a life of deep waters and fierce uncertainty.

"If I weren't so tired, I would throttle you. You deliberately disobeyed me," he spoke in a low, trembling voice.

"I'm sorry."

"Of course. You're always sorry. Why don't you grow up and give me a break?"

He was treating her like a child again. And she deserved it. She nosed into his chest hair and mumbled penitently, "Please don't be angry with me. I just wanted to get a glimpse of the cave. I'm usually surefooted. It was a freak accident."

"Yes, an accident that could have put you on a mortician's slab. How would it look if I delivered you up to your Jeffrey like that? I could always say, 'Sorry, old man. Beastly swimming accident. It wasn't my fault. Your fiancée had a mind of her own. I vowed to take care of her, but she was a stubborn girl.' "

She cringed at his grim humor, but comforted herself with his body. A comfort that didn't last much longer, because he broke away, got up, and slowly walked to the water's edge. He was really disgusted with her. It didn't take a mastermind to figure that out.

She got up to follow him, seeing with a sudden shock that his back was riddled with cuts. In a blinding flash she knew that he had exposed himself to the abrasive rocks in order to shield her.

"Oh, God, Max. What have I done to you?" She touched his back tenderly, and he moved away.

"It's all right."

"But you're bleeding," she sobbed. "All because of me and my stupid curiosity."

"Stop that snivelling," he ordered shortly. "Wash the sand off you, and let's head back. Loa can doctor my back."

He walked slightly ahead of her the whole way back to the house, not speaking, not even looking at her. She felt deeply guilty the whole time, for all she could see was his back. Two of the cuts were about three inches long and quite deep. They were oozing blood.

Guilt mingled with self-pity, and she castigated herself cruelly for ever coming into his life. A man like Max didn't deserve her. If it weren't for her, he wouldn't have taken his plane out before it had been checked over thoroughly, and the engine would have never gone out. His busy life wouldn't have been disrupted by an enforced vacation on Ponsonby's Island. And the time here on the island certainly couldn't have been pleasant, since she was obviously such a nuisance to him. Poor Max. He didn't even have the luxury of being stranded with a woman he could feel a romantic attachment for.

And now this! She looked at his damaged back and shuddered, vowing to herself that she would try desperately to be no more trouble to him in the few short days they had together.

America's most popular, most compelling romance novels...

Here, at last...love stories that really involve you! Fresh, finely crafted novels with story lines so believable you'll feel you're actually living them! Characters you can relate to...exciting places to visit...unexpected plot twists...all in all, exciting romances that satisfy your mind and delight your heart.

EXAMINE 6 LOVESWEPT NOVELS FOR

15 Days FREE!

To introduce you to this fabulous service, you'll get six brand-new Loveswept releases not yet in the bookstores. These six exciting new titles are yours to examine for 15 days without obligation to buy. Keep them if you wish for just $12.50 plus postage and handling and any applicable sales tax.

☐ **YES,** please send me six new romances for a 15-day FREE examination. If I keep them, I will pay just $12.50 (that's six books for the price of five) plus postage and handling and any applicable sales tax and you will enter my name on your preferred customer list to receive all six new Loveswept novels published each month *before* they are released to the bookstores—always on the same 15-day free examination basis.

40311

Name_____

Address_____

City_____

State_____ Zip_____

My Guarantee: I am never required to buy any shipment unless I wish. I may preview each shipment for 15 days. If I don't want it, I simply return the shipment within 15 days and owe nothing for it.

R5234

CHAPTER 6

As they entered the kitchen Loa shrieked, "Mr. Shepherd, what has happened!"

"A swimming mishap," he replied, his eyes darkening with pain and mental anguish.

"Sit down, sit down, sir." Loa pulled out a chair and motioned him into it. Buffy merely looked on in silent helplessness, her legs wobbling visibly, her face beginning to crumple. "You sit, too," Loa ordered her, and Buffy collapsed obediently into a nearby chair.

Max leaned over his knees and shook his head dazedly. Loa gasped as she saw his back. She ran to a cupboard, tsking and fussing as she pulled down a first-aid kit and some antiseptic lotion.

Buffy, apparently acting out the old adage "Confession is good for the soul," began to babble. "Oh, it was all my fault. I walked out on those rocks to see the cave. And fell in," she sniffed. "Max saved me. And the rocks did that to his back." She pointed a trembling finger at the obvious result of her folly.

Loa had begun to wash his cuts with lotion. He clenched his hands in front of him but did not wince. "You went out on those rocks after I warned you about the water?" She turned an accusing gaze on Buffy.

Buffy caught her lower lip between her teeth to keep it from trembling. "Max warned me, too," she said miserably. "I just didn't have any idea the water was so awful until I was right there on top of it."

"You could have both been killed," Loa whispered, horrified. She continued to work deftly with lotion and gauze until she came to the two worst abrasions. "Mr. Shepherd, I will wash these out now. It will hurt." He motioned her to proceed and didn't bat an eye when she poured the liquid into them. "One should have stitches, but I can't do that. I will bring it together, then tape it good," the servant went on, showing great confidence in her nursing abilities. "It will heal right, I promise."

"I trust you," Max said in a low voice. "Go ahead."

Buffy was near the fainting stage now. She was not usually the queasy type, but shock and the sight of Max's blood had taken their toll. She steeled herself against sliding to the floor in a heap, realizing that nobody needed another crisis at this time and that Max was certainly in no condition to pick her up.

"Is there anything I can do to help?" she offered weakly.

"Yes, hold the cut together while I tape," Loa commanded.

She did as she was told, swaying dangerously the whole time, yet glad that she could be of some use.

"I whipped my boys good one time for playing on those rocks," Loa informed her darkly as she finished taping and began to tidy up.

Buffy grasped the back of Max's chair tensely and made an abortive stab at humor. "Max has already tried that method on me once. I guess I'm just a hopeless case."

He rose and looked at her in disgust. "Go on to your room," he ordered shortly. "You need to rest."

She touched his arm. "Can't I help you first?"

"No. Loa will help me. Just go."

He could have just as easily said, "Get out of my sight, I can't stand you." She turned and, as fast as her weakened legs could carry her, she fled to her room, where she cried bitterly.

As a child at the orphanage she had learned to cry silently to keep from disturbing the other homeless girls she roomed with. This was how she cried now. She turned to this almost forgotten method of weeping because she was feeling just as alone and unloved now as she did then.

Tears flowed, but there were no sobs. It was a miserable, lonely way of crying, which befitted the way she felt.

At last she got up, softly blew her nose and dried her eyes, and took a shower. Her knees were skinned slightly and she still felt weak, but compared to Max, she had gotten off easy.

She wrapped herself in her terry-cloth robe and lay down on the bed to stare at the ceiling. She wanted to stay cocooned in this purple room forever. Knowing that Max loathed her was too much to bear.

Loa padded in on silent feet, bearing a tray. "I bring you tea," she said in her musically alto voice. "I already take Mr. Shepherd some. He will be all right," she assured Buffy. She set the tray down on the stand beside the bed and smiled at her.

The overwrought girl was glad that the servant, at least, forgave quickly. "Max hates me," she whispered. "Oh, it's awful, but it's true."

The bed sagged as Loa sat down beside her. "No." She beamed amicably. "Mr. Shepherd loves you."

Buffy covered her eyes with a trembling hand and shook her head.

"Yes, he loves you," Loa insisted, pulling the hand from the tear-ravaged face. "A man," she explained, "he does not show fear like a woman. You frighten Mr. Shepherd when you fall into the water. You frighten him bad. He see you come into his life. Then he see you go under the water. He see all his new happiness maybe lost forever. It make him very mad. He fight to save you. He can not let the waters take you from him. He would die before that. He loves you more than his own life," she finished simply.

Buffy groaned and shook her head again. Loa's interpretation of the incident was too farfetched for comment.

"Have your tea," she spoke gently. "I toast you some fresh raisin bread. Eat it all. Drink all your tea. It will make you strong." She got up to leave. "Mr. Shepherd mad at you because he love you so much."

Loa left the room on that totally illogical note. Buffy sat on the side of the bed and took her tea, feeling somewhat like a pampered invalid. The thick chunk of toast dripping with butter and sprinkled with confectioners' sugar was delicious; the tea, soothing.

Then she lay back down. She was tired, but sleep wouldn't come. She hoped Max was having an easier time resting than she was. Perhaps feeling so guilty about nearly getting herself and Max drowned had something to do with her inability to sleep. Wasn't there a saying "No rest for the wicked"?

She got up restlessly and went to the kitchen, where Loa scolded her softly. "You should be in bed, Miss Buffy."

"I can't sleep. Does Lord Ponsonby have any reading material around here?"

Loa, who was busy arranging deviled eggs on a bed of lettuce, dried her hands on her apron and answered, "There is a study with many books. I never read them, just dust."

"Can't you read, Loa?"

"I never learn. When I was a girl, there was no one to teach. Now," she lifted her apron slightly in a careless gesture, "it no longer important. I very busy. Anyway, I know about life and people, and I know how to love. That is more important. Come, I take you to Boss's study. Many, many books to choose from."

She led Buffy past Max's room, tiptoeing very quietly so as not to disturb him. The very last door along the corridor led into the study.

Late sunshine flowed over amber carpet and a huge oaken desk. Walls were lined from top to bottom with thick leather-bound books. Buffy walked over to examine some of them. They were books of law, all heavy technical volumes. Lord Ponsonby must be an attorney by profession, she surmised.

Loa beamed proudly at being able to present her with such nice fat books. Buffy hadn't the heart to tell her she'd had something more entertaining in mind. A good paperback mystery-thriller, for instance.

"Thank you, Loa. These are nice books. I'm sure I'll find something."

The servant bowed out, leaving Buffy alone to peruse the impressive display. Lord Ponsonby had to have something other than law books in all this.

She began to look for something more her speed. She found some volumes of poetry, but since she felt decidedly unpoetic at the moment, she bypassed these. There was a huge, beautifully bound *Complete Works of Shakespeare*, which she skipped over quickly—she'd had enough of tragedy for one day. And wading through Elizabethan English had been a terrible chore during her high school days. Besides, one could get a hernia lifting the gigantic volume.

She spied a magazine rack and went for it eagerly, hoping for at least one *Ladies' Home Journal* but only finding *Newsweek* and several British publications in the same vein, all outdated.

Finally she discovered a small hard-bound book on a bottom shelf. It was Mark Twain's the *Adventures of Huckleberry Finn*. Oh, well, at least it was American. She doubted if Huckleberry's experiences on the Mississippi could take her mind off her own on Ponsonby's Island; nevertheless, she tucked it under her arm and headed to her room, stepping very lightly past Max's door. She couldn't bear the idea of awakening him and becoming the target of any more of his wrath.

Passing through the kitchen, she waved the book triumphantly at Loa, who in turn looked a little surprised that Buffy had chosen such a thin book compared to all those big, meaty ones she could have selected.

She spent the rest of the afternoon reading about Huck's adventures and, surprisingly, they did get her mind off her own problems, for a while. She remembered that her sixth grade teacher had read the *Adventures of Huckleberry Finn* to the class in daily episodes. But that was so long ago. Now, as an adult reading it afresh, she caught new insights.

Poor Huckleberry was such a young innocent for all his scruffiness. He continually misconstrued and mishandled the people he met and situations in which he found himself. It was the discrepancy between what he thought was true and what was really true that made him such a comical yet endearing figure.

When Loa called her to supper, Buffy dog-eared the page and set the book aside with a sigh. What a charmingly stupid dummy Huckleberry was. Everybody knew the score but him.

She donned her blue pantsuit, did a quick makeup job on her face, which did nothing at all to repair the damage done by tears, and brushed her hair into a beautiful golden halo about her head.

Upon entering the dining room, she saw immediately that the table had been set for only one. At her questioning look, Loa informed her that Max had requested his dinner be brought to his room.

Her heart choked for an instant as she sat down and automatically unfolded her napkin. So, Max couldn't even stand to sit at the same table with her. She thought of their other dinners: the wine, the teasing repartee, the exciting atmosphere that always seemed to surround them when they were together.

She made a pretense of eating but ended up by merely shoving the food from place to place on the old rose china pattern. The gorgeous chicken croquettes might as well have been sawdust. Oh, Max, she thought, please don't hate me forever.

She tried to sip her wine but saw in its rosy depths an image of an attractive, charming gentleman teasing a petite blond woman while they sat at this very table. How he had plied her with wine that first dinner they had shared! He had kissed her hand that night, had held her close while they danced, until she was giddy from more than just the wine.

She set the delicate stemmed glass down without tasting. Memories. She had never before realized how painful they could be. A sudden premonition nearly blotted out her melancholy. If she felt like this now, how would she feel after he was gone out of her life completely? Would she constantly be haunted by sweet, poignant memories of him?

No, of course not. Her life would resume. She would forget about Max and all he had meant to her on Ponsonby's Island. But even as she assured herself, she knew it wasn't so. This infatuation, or whatever it was, would take her a long time to get over.

Loa removed her plate and delivered her dessert, a gorgeous hunk of pecan pie. Her stomach completely revolted at the lovely sight, her chair toppling over as she made for escape.

"Miss Buffy." Loa halted her flight. "Just give him a little time."

"Sure," she said tremulously.

"He didn't eat either," Loa added, as if that knowledge should somehow make her feel better.

"Good night," Buffy bid.

"Good night, honey-girl," the servant wished.

Buffy's dreams were haunted by water that night. She must have dreamed the near tragedy over and over in various versions. Max was always reaching for her and not quite connecting. He wanted to tell her something, but waves of water kept crashing between them.

She awoke, her body damp with icy perspiration. It was the middle of the night. The water she had heard in her dreams was real, for rain was coming down in fierce, driving blankets. She got out of bed and walked to the window, which was being lit up like a neon sign every few seconds by lightning.

She stepped back from the sight and the sound, clutching her fists to her temples. This was all she needed to top off a perfectly disastrous day. It was the cherry on the whipped cream, the icing on the cake. The tropical storm, her old childhood bogeyman, had come to add his crashing orchestration to this terrible day of nightmares.

She ran to the bed and ducked in. Covers were her only defense. Why was she so uncommonly frightened of storms? One should surely outgrow such a childish phobia. Perhaps it was because she never had anyone to run to, no one to assure her it was only a storm, that it would pass. She wondered if she would always be alone and afraid of storms. Would there ever be anyone to offer her comfort and assurance when it was needed?

She shivered and listened. The noisy thrashing on the roof suddenly ceased, as was the way with tropical deluges. There were a few intermittent spatters and then nothing. She pulled the comforter from her head, turned on the bedside lamp, and let out a deep, tremulous sigh. Reaching for the *Adventures of Huckleberry Finn,* she settled down into the bedclothes and lost herself in Huck's foolish antics for fifteen minutes. Then she turned off the light and fell asleep again, this time dreamlessly.

In an effort to dispel the cloud of depression that hovered over her the next morning, she decided to take a nice lengthy jog. There is nothing like intense physical exercise to brighten one's outlook, she reasoned.

In less than twenty minutes she was clipping down the beach in her bikini at a steady pace, her bare feet making regular but barely audible slapping sounds against the wet sand. She drew great draughts of salt-tanged air into her lungs, and soon life-giving oxygen had set her whole body aglow—a slim, taut body that glistened with a thin sheen of perspiration.

It was still quite early and she saluted a new sun rising over the water. Her vision delighted in the shiny bronze waves that regularly touched the sand, and her ears rang with the screeching of lonely gulls overhead. Little sandpipers darted in a mad scramble to get out of her way as she stepped up her pace, running ecstatically into a pungently intoxicating breeze laced with a fishy, salty smell.

Beach jogging was a sensual experience. The sights and sounds and smells of the sea and sand were exquisite. Her body moved as one with the elements. As she ran into what she figured was her second mile, she became almost airborne. Firm, smooth legs moved effortlessly; arms and shoulders relaxed; breathing became automatically precise.

Approaching the black rocks of the cave, she turned into a field of sparse sea oats and traversed the diameter of the island. Upon reaching the other side, she again jogged the beach.

The sun was bright now and getting hot. Rivulets of sweat streamed down her neck and between her breasts. She wondered fleetingly if any of Max's lady friends, Marlene, for instance, ever worked up a good, honest, sweet-smelling sweat—or even if they knew that perspiration brought on by extreme physical exertion is practically odorless and works like a marvelous sauna for the entire body. No, she decided, Marlene and her set were too sophisticated to run themselves gloriously into the dawn of a new day.

She must have jogged nearly four miles by now. Logical thought became impossible. The motor side of her brain had taken over—the reasoning side completely shutting down. It was a blessed relief. She became a creature of mere motion instead of thought, somewhat like primitive woman.

Reaching the path strewn with pine straw, which led to the house, she stopped running and began to walk. Her breathing quickly returned to normal, but she still sweated profusely. She knew from experience that she would continue to do so for about ten minutes. She swept it out of her eyes and walked at a leisurely pace toward the house, feeling buoyantly free. One of the best things about running was stopping: it felt so good.

She went straight to the pool and took a leaping dive into its blue refreshment. When she surfaced, she saw Max standing on the deck, glowering at her.

Oh, no, he's still mad, she thought. "Hi." She waved.

"Where the devil have you been?" he blazed. "Get out of there." He strode over to the edge, every taut movement indicating barely suppressed fury.

He extended a hand to her, and she didn't mince around in allowing him to pull her out. "How's your back today?" she asked, shaking her wet curls with her hands.

"I asked you where you'd been," he menaced, ignoring her solicitous inquiry concerning his health.

"Running," she answered innocently.

"And you didn't care how I might worry about you, wondering if you were off somewhere drowning yourself? Couldn't you have at least left a note or given someone a message as to your whereabouts?"

She stiffened defiantly. She was fed up with Max's moody anger and overbearing manner. "I don't have to answer to you or anybody, Max. I've been taking care of myself for years."

His lips pressed together in a thin white line, and as she made a move to pass him, he grabbed her arm and stuck a forefinger under her nose. "Let's get something straight, shall we?" he ground out in low, clipped tones. "As long as we're here, you answer to me. I have no intentions of going through any more hell getting you out of trouble." His voice lowered a degree in pitch as his grip on her arm tightened to the threshold of outright pain. "Don't ever go out alone again without telling me or Loa. That's an order." He released her abruptly.

"Don't bully me, Max," she warned. "I don't need all this chauvinistic domination. I don't need it, and I don't want it."

"I'll tell you what you need, my feisty little brat. You need someone to make a woman of you. I doubt if young Dunstan is capable of it."

"And I suppose you are?" She saw him flinch and figured she'd gained an advantage in the battle, although for the world she couldn't imagine why. Nevertheless, she intended to make full use of it.

She flounced around saucily in front of him in her tempting white bikini, not realizing the provocative figure she was cutting. "Come on, Max. Could you do it? Could the proper English gentleman make a poor little scruffy orphan into a woman?" She sashayed toward him seductively. "What's the first step?" she taunted childishly in his face. "A kiss? Come on," she sneered, "are you too much a gentleman, or are you just not man enough? Make me a woman, Max. I dare you."

The gauntlet had been thrown down; the glove had been

slapped across the face. It was a challenge no man, least of all the virile Max Shepherd, could ignore. A glitter of determination silvered his eyes; a mirthless smile curled his lips. All of a sudden Buffy realized she had been courting fire.

He grabbed her shoulders and roughly pulled her into his chest, his mouth coming down on hers in a wide, biting kiss. He parted her lips savagely and plundered the sweetness of her mouth without compunction, taking all a man's pleasure from it.

A little helpless cry died in her throat and became a moan as his hands slid from her shoulders to her waist and then cupped under her buttocks, where they drew her upward into the sheer virility of him.

By now her senses were whirling dizzily and her legs, already weak from running, completely gave way. She clung to his muscular shoulders, becoming as putty in his hands.

She gave a little half sob into his mouth as he moved her hips suggestively against his fully aroused body and continued to ravish her mouth mercilessly.

A primitive and strangely beautiful fire licked through her veins, and she became confused as wave upon wave of painful yearning seared her body.

Finally he yielded his hold somewhat; his kiss lessened in intensity. But he continued to play with her lips until she sobbed, "Please. Oh, please, stop."

He let her down gently and held her until she found her legs. She sagged against him, trying to pull herself together.

When she looked up, she saw him regarding her through two narrow silver slits. Helpless vulnerability shone all over her face.

"There," he whispered. "You've gone and taunted me into doing something I had no intentions of doing."

He was so calm about it all, while she was nearly shaking to pieces. He set her away from him, balancing her gently, as if she were a porcelain figurine.

"I'm sorry. You weren't ready for that," he murmured

107

softly. Then he laid a chaste kiss on her damp brow and left her swaying back and forth slightly.

Eventually she was able to shamble to her room. After changing out of her suit and into her robe, she sat immobile on the edge of the bed for what seemed like an eternity, her hands clasped dumbly in her lap.

She had asked for it. She had asked for everything he had so expertly shown her. Oh, the sheer folly of challenging a man like Max! Wouldn't she ever learn? He had vanquished her just as surely as he had the day he beat her at tennis and then spanked her for flying into him. Only this time his method had been even more devastating.

She trembled in confusion and shame as she recalled that unreality she experienced when he had kissed her, the sheer helplessness of losing herself in the taste and feel of him. Max must be the only man in the world who kissed like that. He paled Jeffrey's feeble gropings into pasty nothingness. Jeffrey had never set her on fire as Max had just done, nor had he ever left her so jumbled up emotionally.

Oh, well, what did it all mean? Only that he'd punished her tauntings with a kiss that he hadn't wanted to give and that she was in no way prepared to receive. She had wanted him to kiss her on the beach. Now he had, and very thoroughly. The memory of the overpowering sexuality of it caused her to shiver.

Max was an unknown element, and one naturally feared the unknown. She was frightened of her unreasonable attraction to him. If she didn't watch herself, she might even fall in love with him, which would be disastrous, for there was no future in it. After all, he felt nothing for her. He hadn't even wanted to kiss her. She had goaded him into it. He had admitted as much.

They ate lunch inside, since the wind was blustering and it was threatening to rain. He was more like his old self now, his anger toward her over the near drowning apparently having evaporated in the heat of their kiss. Yet there was a certain restless tenseness under all his charm, which she could not account for.

"More fruit, Buffy?" he asked politely, passing her the bowl.

"Thank you." She served herself from it and ate without relish. "Max," she began hesitantly, "I've made up my mind not to be any more trouble to you." She stabbed at a slice of banana that evaded her and that she had no appetite to pursue.

"That's awfully considerate of you, Buffy," he said in a light, teasing tone.

"No, I mean it," she averred. "I got you into all this. If it hadn't been for me, your plane would have gotten properly overhauled and your engine wouldn't have burned out and you wouldn't be stuck here on this island with me and you wouldn't have mangled up your back and nearly drowned . . ." she ended breathlessly. "A-and I know that kiss was my fault, too."

He sat calmly stirring his coffee, smiling at her with those icy gray eyes, saying nothing. She noted his sensuous lips, his strong, sinewy hands. The full memory of the kiss came back to her with such force that she felt as if she'd been kicked in the stomach. Her lips parted and she closed her eyes recalling her disturbing, yet somehow beautiful, responses to him.

She swallowed thickly and when she opened her eyes, she saw his teeth flashing into a knowing grin. She stuck her nose in the air, silently wondering if telepathy was another one of his unusual gifts. He gave a deep, attractive chuckle, and she knew he was aware of how much his passionate kiss had shaken her. Oh, drat the man and his self-assured arrogance!

"Well!" she breathed exasperatedly.

"Well what?" he asked, sipping his coffee complaisantly. "Are you trying to tell me how deep your thoughts are?"

"Very funny," she said stiffly. "I was just wondering . . ." She searched around for something to wonder about other than Max. ". . . why the weather is so foul," she finally lit upon. "It's not normal for this time of year. I'm not sure about here in the islands, but September in Florida is usually heavenly. Just like spring. As a matter of fact, I always got spring fever in the fall of the year." He nodded as if he expected something like this from her. "Just about the time I got about a month into the new school year, it would hit me. The sun would cool a little, the breeze would blow the palm trees tantalizingly, and every blade of grass seemed to be calling me to the tennis courts."

"And did you go?" he asked.

"Credit me with a little sense, Max. I was a well-known tennis ace even at that age. I would never do anything that would jeopardize my reputation. Getting into trouble for skipping school wouldn't have done my career a bit of good." She smiled mischievously. "But believe me, I wanted to."

"I'll bet you gave your teachers one helluva time," he commented, leaning back in his chair and lighting up a cheroot.

"And I'll bet you were a model child," she retorted. "A regular little Lord Fauntleroy." A picture of a miniature Max in short breeches and knee socks skipped across her brain and nearly threw her into gales of laughter. "I'll bet you went to the finest prep schools England has to offer," she jibed sarcastically.

"Indeed I did," he admitted, not the least bit ruffled. "My dear mother insisted upon it. Although I daresay she would take issue with you over my being a model student."

"And of course you're an Oxford man," she continued in a sarcastic voice.

"Naturally." He puffed his cheroot and looked down his nose at her on purpose.

"Well, I'm sorry I can't claim to be a Rhodes scholar," she snapped, "but I've been too busy just surviving. I *have* taken a few courses at Miami University, though, for fun."

"I don't suggest that you become an intellectual, Buffy,"

Max cut in. "It would totally ruin you. You're quite exciting just as you are."

"In other words, you like me dumb," she said pointedly.

He looked extremely amused. "Let's just say I find your sort of brave freshness rather invigorating. One never knows quite what to expect from one moment to the next with you, my darling." He leaned forward and clasped her hand warmly.

"What kind of backhanded compliment is that?" she asked.

He rubbed his fingers across her hand, making it feel like a well-stabbed pincushion. Little prickles radiated from his point of contact, up her arm, and threatened to move into more vital areas before she tore her hand away.

"I'm only telling you how fascinating you are. Most women love to hear that sort of thing," he remarked.

"I wasn't aware that you even considered me a woman," she countered.

"Sometimes I do." His eyes became hooded and unreadable.

Buffy rose from the table, excused herself politely, and thanked Loa for the lunch. After staying in her room for about twenty minutes, she became so restless that she soon was prowling around like a caged feline. Since it had already started to rain, playing tennis or doing anything else outside was out of the question. She was too wide awake to take a nap. And she'd already finished the *Adventures of Huckleberry Finn*.

She picked up the book and traipsed down the plushy carpeted hall toward the study. The door to Max's room was wide open. She swiveled her head around and got a good look while sailing by, then halted and backed up a few steps. Max wasn't in his room.

She stood at the door of the empty room for about as long as it took Pandora to decide to open the forbidden box. Woman's curiosity had its way, and she began a slow, furtive amble into Max's bedroom, whistling tunelessly as if she were quite unaware that she was an uninvited, and probably unwanted, guest.

She saw that his imprint was still in the black velvet spread; he'd evidently rested for a few minutes just after lunch. Still humming, she straightened the spread. It gave her an excuse to wander even deeper into his private territory.

She touched things—lampshades, furniture surfaces, bric-a-brac. A very nice room it was, she decided. She circled around and casually peeked into the bathroom.

There were Max's shaving things all laid out, and that tangy lime cologne he wore. Max was a neat man. On the other hand, he wasn't fastidious. One could tell that by the way he hung up his towels. She shuffled into the room to straighten the towels. And here was his shirt just slung over the doorknob. She grabbed the shirt so that she could hang it up for him. It was the black silky one he wore so often. She paused over it, then quite ridiculously raised it to her cheek, the masculine scent of him filling the air she breathed and making her suddenly dizzy.

"Do you go around hugging empty shirts all the time?" Max asked from behind her.

"Oh! What are you doing here?" Buffy spun around crazily.

"This is my room, remember? More specifically, my bathroom." He leaned against the doorjamb and folded his arms over his chest.

She rolled her eyes and groaned in embarrassment. She thought of a couple of lies she could use to explain why she was in his bathroom, but they would make her present situation even more ridiculous. Max would never believe Loa had sent her here to check the plumbing or to fetch dirty clothes.

He continued to watch her calmly, and she knew her face must be glowing iridescently. Finally she took a deep breath and told the truth. "Max, I don't know what I'm doing here." She put her hands on her hips and faced him squarely, glad to see that he didn't look at all angry. "I was just on my way to the study. And I saw your door open—"

"No need to apologize," he broke in.

112

"Well, I am sorry. I have no right to be in here."

"It's perfectly all right. You're welcome anytime." He was being gentlemanly to a ridiculous degree, and they both knew it.

"Thank you," she said stupidly. "And here's your shirt."

"Thank you," he said, grinning as he took it.

"I straightened a couple of your hand towels." She nodded to the towel bar.

"That was kind of you." By now he was twinkling, and her cheeks were positively scorching.

"Would you let me pass?" she asked politely.

"Of course." He jumped out of her way gallantly.

She riveted her eyes straight ahead and walked out of his bathroom with what she hoped was aplomb. She could feel his dancing gray eyes on her the whole time and knew he was not far behind her as she crossed the bronze carpet to his bedroom door.

"I was just going to the study, myself," he said. "To do a bit of work. How coincidental that we're both headed in the same direction." He laughed.

He was making fun; she could tell by the uptilt of one side of his mouth.

"Yes." She blinked sweetly, trying not to rise to his bait. "What a coincidence."

They entered the study together, and she saw that papers were scattered on the broad desk top. Max had apparently been doing some figuring of some sort.

"I didn't know you had brought work with you," she commented.

"I didn't really," he said, taking a seat behind the desk. "I've just taken this rainy-day opportunity to figure out a few things concerning our South Caicos resort." He held out his hand and asked, "What book are you reading there?"

"I've already read it." She handed it to him reluctantly and watched him smile secretly before handing it back to her.

113

"And what did you think of young Huckleberry?" he asked.

She moved to the corner to put the book where it belonged. "I think he was too innocent to cope with the situations in which he found himself."

"How true." He sat back and lit a cheroot.

"But he had plenty of spirit along with all that innocence," she said. "You have to admire him for that."

"Oh, yes," he agreed, a deep light kindling his eyes. "One would have to admire a person like that."

"You know," she said, walking back over to the desk and perching herself on top of it, "I think Mark Twain must have had a wonderful marriage."

"Why do you say that?"

"Well, there was a biographical note at the beginning of the book, which told about his personal life and gave some of his thoughts and sayings. He said of his wife, 'Where she is, there is Eden.' Isn't that beautiful?"

"Lovely. What's so unusual about it?"

"Max," she explained, "he said that about her after they had been married for decades."

"So? True love doesn't fade away when the honeymoon is over. It's not inconceivable to me that the man still loved his wife so much after he grew old and developed that shock of bushy white hair and that outrageous handlebar mustache."

"But that kind of romantic love doesn't live through years of marriage. Romance, if it exists at all, dies when the problems of daily living set in." She sat, in her expensive well-tailored suit, with her legs dangling off the edge of the desk, a curious mixture of woman and child.

"You're wrong, Buffy. Mark Twain wouldn't have called his wife a Garden of Eden if he didn't mean it." He looked down and began doodling on a map of some sort. "And remind me to tell you about my parents someday."

"Why, Max!" she exclaimed, craning her neck to look at the map. "That looks like one of those hurricane-tracking maps they give out free at the radio and television stations in Florida."

"It is. Pons orders one every season. See, here's the longitudinal and latitudinal lines."

"Oh, yes." She jumped off the desk and curled herself over the map in one lithe movement, jangling her charm bracelet and filling the air with the clean scent of herself as she did so. She pointed at a little cyclonic-looking symbol and tapped it thoughtfully with her pink fingernail. "And there's the hurricane." There's the hurricane? She froze into a statue.

"Yes," he agreed. "There's the hurricane."

The full implication of the map sank in. "Really! There's really a hurricane out there?"

"Yes. The low pressure area developed into a bona fide hurricane last night. Myaka and I have been keeping track of the situation for a couple of days. It's one hundred miles wide and moving at about twenty miles an hour. Force winds are about seventy-five miles an hour."

She closed her eyes and asked, "Why didn't you tell me sooner?"

"We didn't want to worry you and Loa."

"When will it hit?" she asked, somewhat like a terminal cancer patient asks a doctor how many more days he has to live.

"We really don't know if it will hit us. See"—he pointed—"it's just north of the Domincan Republic now. The last report had it coming this way. But you know how unpredictable these storms are."

She clenched her teeth and uttered an unintelligible sound.

"Buffy," he chided softly. "You can't be that frightened. Living in Florida, you have to have gone through a couple of hurricanes in your life."

"Two," she informed him in a high, watery voice, but didn't add how each one had been her own private hell. She was fourteen when she experienced the last one. Mr. Johnson had finally resorted to fixing her a hot toddy out of his best medicinal whiskey in order to calm her down.

"Well, then, you know what to expect. Myaka and I are keeping track of it, and if it doesn't veer off within the

115

next couple of hours, I'm afraid we'll have to take precautions. But it will be hours before it hits us, if it does at all."

She smiled at him rather vacantly and prayed silently that it would blow itself somewhere millions of miles away from Ponsonby's Island. And if by chance it didn't, she asked fervently that she wouldn't become the hysterical female that she had become when she was fourteen. After all, it was time for her to grow up where the subject of storms was concerned.

CHAPTER 7

By noon the next day, Max and Myaka were busy battening down everything on the island. There was a driving rain, and the surf was riotous. The hurricane was due to hit Ponsonby's Island in the evening. Buffy held herself bravely, but her eyes wore a hunted look that nobody seemed to notice, for everybody had a part to do in preparing for the storm.

"Miss Buffy," Loa asked, "will you help me fold up the patio furniture and put it away in the utility room?"

"Sure," Buffy agreed stiffly. This physical action helped to take her mind off the horror of what was coming. "Where's Max and Myaka?" she asked through the rain as she snapped porch chairs into flat positions.

"Making sure boat tied up good. Putting plane in hangar." She gazed up into the driving rain pensively. "They will have to bring plywood from garage next and board up windows." She motioned to the plate glass windows facing the pool.

Buffy had a sudden vision of all the glass shattering into a million crystal splinters. "How bad will it be, Loa?"

"Sometimes they are bad, and sometimes it's all just a lot of work for nothing. This one may be very bad. My man say wind will get worse as it comes over water. But it will hit Andros Island before us. Maybe that will knock some breath out of it. Seven years ago big hurricane called Milly emptied the pool into the living room. That was when sunken living rooms were in style. Boss made big joke about us having a real sunken living room."

"Lord Ponsonby must have quite a sense of humor,"

commented Buffy stiffly as she imagined the horror of having one's pool washed into one's living room.

"Boss see fun in everything. My man say it his way of getting through sadness in life. His wife, she die a long time ago. He give Marlene everything. She disappoint him many times. She no good." Loa said this as she and Buffy dragged a patio table into the utility room and walked back out to the poolside for another.

"I sure hope the pool doesn't come into the house this time," Buffy murmured worriedly.

"No, it won't," Loa assured her easily. "After last time, my man make plywood shutters to fit windows. My man and Mr. Shepherd will have them up soon. They will also drain some water out of pool before storm. Everything will be okay."

They had finished storing the furniture and several hanging planters when Max and Myaka walked up.

"You two shouldn't have done this," Max protested. "Myaka and I were going to make the patio our next job."

"You had better get those shutters up," Buffy warned.

"Yes, we had," said Max, slapping Myaka on the shoulder convivially.

She noticed that everyone, except herself, seemed to be taking the impending danger in stride. Max was in an almost carnival mood. She trembled as dampness and fear drove into her very bones.

"You're shivering," Max said to her. "You and Loa go on inside and fill up the tubs and sinks with water. We'll need a supply. After I turn off the generator, the pump won't run."

"I've already taken care of water supply, Mr. Shepherd," Loa said. "But I think I'll go in and fix you and Miss Buffy a real fine dinner, plenty of cold cuts and salads."

Buffy followed Loa inside, both of them taking off their slickers and hanging them in the utility room. She wondered how on earth everyone had caught this strange party spirit. A hurricane was coming—weren't they afraid?

"Within the next hour my man and I will be leaving for

our house," Loa informed her as they walked into the kitchen together. "You and Mr. Shepherd will look after things here." She tied an apron around her and began to pull the makings for salad out of the refrigerator. "I fix you plenty to eat, since generator will be off and you won't have way to cook."

"I doubt if I'll be very hungry, anyway," Buffy remarked in a high, forced voice.

"Oh, sure," Loa said. "All you can do during a hurricane is eat. Eat and sleep. And make love." She gave Buffy a mischievous glance.

Buffy gave her a squelching look and began to shred lettuce. She knew for certain she wouldn't be doing any of those things, least of all the last. It would probably be all she could do just to keep from screaming her head off.

Loa flipped the light on when Max and Myaka set the shutter in the kitchen window and nailed it on. Within an hour they had every window in Ponsonby's Palace shuttered tightly. It was like a tomb.

Then the lights went out, throwing them in darkness. Loa fumbled for a butane lamp and soon had it going. It cast an eerie glow about the kitchen.

"Generator is off," Loa announced brightly. "Mr. Shepherd will make sure it's secure and well protected before coming in." She examined with satisfaction the array of food, then slipped off her apron and went into the utility room to put on a slicker. "I'll go home now. My man wait for me. He say after Mr. Shepherd turn off generator, to come."

Max entered as she was leaving. "Take care, Loa," he said. "Everything at your house is shipshape, too. We took care of it this morning."

Loa nodded and smiled, and the wind whipped her out the door. Max pushed the door shut and shrugged out of his slicker and then out of his sopping tennis shoes.

"Well," he said, smiling at Buffy, who stood looking at him dumbly, "we've done all we can do. Now we sit it out."

"About how high is the wind now?" she asked.

"Only about thirty-five miles an hour," he answered. "The storm should be hitting Andros about now. It's impossible to get anything on the radio; there's too much interference. But I estimate she'll hit us around eight o'clock tonight with winds well over 100 mph."

He walked over to the food-laden counter and popped an hors d'oeuvre in his mouth and munched on it while he poured himself a glass of white wine. He sipped on it while he ate a shrimp, then a cream cheese hors d'oeuvre.

"Mmm. Drinking wine and eating hors d'oeuvres. Can't think of a better way to go." His dark wet hair hung forward and was dripping intermittently, but he seemed altogether happy.

Buffy gasped, "What do you mean, you can't think of a better way to go!" His fatalistic teasing had completely unnerved her.

"Well, I can think of at least one way that's better, actually." He licked his thumb and gave her a wink.

"Oh, Max!" she said exasperatedly. "How can you joke at a time like this? We are in danger. Am I the only one who realizes it?"

He moved casually toward her. "I've secured us in here quite well, luv," he assured her. "Ponsonby called early this morning from Madrid. I didn't understand a lot of what he said, due to the bad connection, but I did gather that he feels this house is virtually hurricane-proof since he had Myaka build the shutters. I drained the pool halfway, so there's no danger of it's water being blown under the glass sliding doors. We're too high up to be hit by tidal waves. So what's your problem? We're cocooned in here. Safe. Don't you believe me? Trust me?"

At that point she nearly told him about her unreasonable fear of storms, about never having anyone to run to as a child when the winds would blow. But she stood erect and quite deliberately decided not to. It would only make her more a child in his eyes. And she couldn't bear to be reduced anymore than she already was.

"I-I guess I'm just nervous."

He took a cream cheese hors d'oeuvre and knocked on

her chin with his forefinger. She opened her mouth obediently, and he popped it in. "There. What you need is food and wine and"—he smiled slyly; her eyes widened in alarm—"and gin rummy."

"Wh-what?" she asked, trying to pry cream cheese off the roof of her mouth with her tongue. Her nerves had made her mouth much too dry to masticate anything, least of all anything gooey.

"Gin rummy." He laughed, turning her toward her room. "Go on and get into something comfortable, then I'll beat you soundly at cards."

She washed in the water Loa had trapped in the sink in her bathroom, then donned a soft white lounge dress. It zipped up the front and had a yoke of ice-blue embroidered flowers.

She carried the lantern Max had given her over to the closet-door mirror and held it up to look at herself. A frightened waiflike child stared back at her—a child who had lost her way or who had awakened from a terrifying dream.

It would never do for Max to see her in this condition. She set the lantern on the dresser and went to work on her face with cosmetics. A touch of blusher, some bright lipstick, did wonders. But there was nothing to be done about her overly large liquid-amber eyes, which mirrored a haunted look of childish fear. She would just have to put on a brave front. Max must never know how frightened she was. It would only confirm his opinion that she was still a baby. What woman at twenty fell to pieces during a storm, for heaven's sake?

She walked into the dining room, a brave little ghost. Max was sitting at the table, dressed casually in tan jeans and a knit pullover, open at the neck, shuffling cards like a professional.

"I warn you, Max." She smiled too brightly. "I used to be the champion rummy player in the dorm at the orphanage."

"Ah, you are forever challenging me, aren't you, luv?"

"I can't help it." She laughed hollowly, going into the

kitchen to get the wine and a plate of food. "I guess it's the competitive spirit in me." She set the food on the table and poured them each a glass of wine.

"Have you ever wondered what it would be like if you didn't have to fight, if you didn't have to constantly struggle?"

"Oh, yes. But I imagine I'll reach that happy state when I'm in heaven. Life has always been a struggle for me, and I'm sure it will continue to be."

"But there are little spots of heaven on earth, you know." He began to flip them each cards like a Las Vegas dealer.

"Well, if there are," she countered, picking up her cards, "I haven't run across any of them yet."

"Perhaps you will soon." He smiled.

"That would be nice." The hurricane outside had risen to a dull roar. She played her cards with sweaty hands. "I wonder what it's doing out there," she said tremulously.

"Let's go see," he suggested, lifting up one of the lanterns from the table and holding out a hand to her. "I left the shutter off the utility room window so we could check the progress of the storm from time to time. The panes of that window are so small that I doubt they could shatter. Come on," he urged, "let's go look. I'm curious, myself."

The view from the small window did nothing at all to reassure her that she would live through the night. Palm trees were bent double. One giant oak next to the house was listing heavily. Droplets of water whipped through the air and sprayed against the glass like gravel.

"What time is it?" she asked.

"Seven o'clock," he answered from behind her.

"It's like this already, and the storm hasn't even hit us full force yet!"

"It will get worse," he said softly and put his hands on her shoulders. "Come away now."

It wasn't long before the hurricane hit with great intensity. It sounded like an ever-present freight train going overhead. Buffy and Max continued to play rummy. She sipped a great deal of wine and talked too nervously, too brightly.

"I warned you I was an expert at cards," she said over the storm. "Gin!" She laid her cards down triumphantly.

"This is getting to be monotonous. How many times have you beat me?"

"I've lost count."

He cocked his head and listened attentively to an ominous creaking noise. "It's the roof," he explained to her. "They have to give a little in a storm like this."

She shuffled the cards with trembling fingers, all the while expecting the roof to fly off. One part of her brain talked and played cards; another coiled tighter and tighter into barely controlled hysteria.

"So," she said as she dealt cards, "tell me about your work."

"You already know it." He put his hand to his mouth and stifled a yawn. "I own hotels."

"Tell me about the new one. Where did you say it was going to be?"

"South Caicos. It's one of the Grand Turk Islands, which is a part of the British West Indies. The islands in the Grand Turks are not as large as many of those in the Bahamas, but they are every bit as beautiful, perhaps more so."

"How far away is it?"

"Nearly six hundred miles; it lies about halfway between Miami and Puerto Rico."

"What's your hotel there going to be like?"

"We are designing it along the order of Ponsonby's Paradise. Our guests will stay in a complex of individual bungalows, very modern, like Pons has here." He put his hand to his mouth again and this time he actually did yawn. "Sorry. Where was I? Oh, yes. We will have a casino, a huge restaurant. Tennis, of course." He bowed toward her deferentially. "A pool. Like the one at the Polynesian Village at Disney World in Orlando. Have you seen it?"

"Yes."

123

"All those rocks, caves, and waterfalls. Marvelous!"

"Golf?"

"We don't want to take up space putting in a golf course. Besides, our guests will probably mostly be sports fishermen. South Caicos has a natural yacht basin. Most of our guests, probably all, as a matter of fact, will come by yacht. It will be a paradise for the very wealthy."

"I suppose you own a yacht."

"Yes, I'll live on it while the new resort is being built."

"You're an impressive man, Max."

He yawned again and made a noise something like a bear getting ready to go into hibernation.

"For heaven's sake, are you really that sleepy?" she asked incredulously. "I don't see how in the world you could be yawning from boredom with that raging storm going on outside."

"Don't you feel it?" he asked equally incredulous.

"Feel what, for heaven's sake?" All she felt was the adrenaline of fear pumping through her veins like quicksilver. She probably wouldn't be able to sleep for forty years.

"The atmosphere, it has grown heavy. It makes one want to fall asleep. I always sleep like a log during a hurricane. I rather think it's the drop in the barometric pressure which causes this condition, but that's just a theory. . . ." Then he actually dozed off sitting right at the table.

She slapped her cards down and reached over and shook him. "Wake up!" she hissed.

"Wh-what? Did you beat me again?"

"No, Max. But I will, literally, if you don't stay awake and keep an eye on this place."

"Okay, okay." He held up a tired hand. "Let's go over and sit on the couch, though. At least it's more comfortable there."

He lumbered over to the couch and collapsed in a sprawl, while she quickly cleared the table and made a beeline for him before he drifted off into dreamland.

Tucking her legs under her and arranging the long white dress around her modestly, she ordered, "Tell me about your childhood, right from the beginning."

He regarded her from sleepy gray eyes, which seemed to contain a wealth of unexpressed emotion. "You look like a little satin flower in that thing." He flicked one of the white cap sleeves with a forefinger.

Just then the roof creaked again, and she had to hold herself stiffly to keep from running through the house like a raving maniac. "Your mother," she smiled at him. "Tell me about her."

He leaned back on Ponsonby's wide plush couch and looked toward the ceiling. "She was small and fine-boned like you. But delicate. She died six years ago in her sleep. About five o'clock in the morning. A heart attack."

"Oh, I'm so sorry, Max. I didn't know your mother was no longer living. Even though I didn't see anyone with your father at Palm Isle, I certainly didn't know he was a widower."

"It's quite all right, Buffy," he assured her. "Every time I think of mother, they are happy thoughts. She may have been weak in health, but she was a giant in spirit. Impulsive, like you. She led both Dad and me a merry chase. We adored her."

"I suppose you miss her very much."

"At times, yes. Actually, I was off to school in England a great deal of the time, so I learned to live without her before she died. Dad took it very hard, though. He still hasn't come out of it completely. Talks at times about going to be with her."

"That's morbid talk," Buffy protested.

Max looked down at his hands. "Yes, I know, but you see, he loved her so very much. She was part of him—flesh of his flesh, bone of his bone. When she died, a very vital part of him died, too."

"But he still has you."

"Yes, I think that's what keeps him alive. He's got me and the business. He's still an ambitious man for all his years. He loves to send me off to build new hotels, like the one at Caicos. I am an architect by profession. He takes great pride in that."

125

Buffy curled toward him like a white persian kitten and played with a lock of her hair. "I understand why you believe in love. If I'd have had parents, perhaps I would know more. Perhaps I would really be in love with Jeffrey and not just engaged to him."

"No," he ground out. "You wouldn't be in love with Jeffrey at this moment."

"Probably not," she sighed. "Oh, when will this storm end? The noise just goes on and on."

"The eye will pass over soon," he remarked sluggishly. "When it does, we will have about thirty minutes of silence. During that time I want you to go to bed. It will give you time to get to sleep before the other side hits us."

Buffy had no intentions of going to bed, of going to her room to hide under her covers, of lying defenseless while wind took the roof off and water washed over her in torrents.

"Why haven't you ever married, Max?" she asked.

Silence suddenly thundered around them; the absence of the wind was deafening. "The eye," he explained.

"You didn't answer my question." She tried to pin him down. But he was already getting up.

Oh, please don't leave me, she cried silently. The storm will come back and I'll be alone. "Come on," she coaxed. "You're over thirty. You believe in love, yet you're not married. Why?"

"The answer is obvious." He penetrated her with his silver gaze, then turned away wearily.

"Don't tell me a man of your sophistication hasn't yet met the woman he could marry," she goaded. "There must have been dozens of women in your life."

"There were, but none I could love until—" He stopped and ran a hand over dark silky waves. "Go to bed, Buffy." He left then, very quickly and very decisively, taking one of the lanterns with him.

Until what? she wondered. Being a normal female, she didn't cotton to unanswered questions. And whenever one presented itself, she immediately provided her own answer to it. Until Marlene, she decided. He loves Marlene and is going to marry her.

She took her own lantern and walked to her room. She didn't like the answer she'd come up with, but there was no other. "Until. . . ." He'd dropped it off. Until Marlene, who else? It was logic, pure and simple.

She wandered nervously around her room, wondering when the other side of the storm would hit. She decided to take the lantern into the kitchen and wash up some dishes. It would give her something to do.

After washing the few dishes in water Loa had trapped in the sink, she set them on the drainer to dry. She then covered the leftover food and put it in the refrigerator, which was still cold, even though it wasn't running.

Taking the lantern, she walked into the utility room to look out the window. It was deadly calm, and she could actually see stars twinkling in the sky. She set the lantern on the floor and rested her elbows on the windowsill. She'd never been in the eye of a hurricane before. She knew, though, that when the winds hit again, they would be coming from the other direction and their force would be just as terrific as if the lull had never occurred.

She moved back from the window in sudden premonition, and all hell broke loose. Glass shattered, wind whipped through her hair, water sprayed her face, and a horrible monster poked its black wet arms through the broken windowpanes.

Hysteria sprang from its tightly wound position, and she crouched and screamed and screamed, and she knew she'd go on doing so for the rest of her life.

Even when Max pulled a patio table across the window, she still held her head and screamed. When he backed her out of the utility room and closed the door, she screamed on and on. It was only when he lifted her gently into his arms and carried her to his bed that her screams died into dry, uncontrollable sobs.

He hushed her and held her close. "The oak tree," he crooned. "It was only the oak tree. It blew over and broke

127

the window. It was nothing. Don't cry, pet. Don't be frightened."

He went on and on soothing her, calling her little love names. He cupped her face and showered it with kisses, buried his hands and face in her hair, gathered her close and held her tightly.

She calmed, and the wonder of where she was and what he was doing flushed through her like a warm fire. He was calling her his baby, his lovely. His kisses were chasing the fear away. His body was giving her comfort, protection. She snuggled into him greedily. He was a luxury she'd never before known—this safety, this love in the middle of the night when all the outside world was a raging storm.

The masculine sweetness of his lips so freely given, his wide, gentle arms, the virile strength of his body, his soft cooings of assurance, were like an anchor, a rock to cling to.

"I've been so frightened," she whispered into his muscular shoulder.

"I know. I saw your fear, and I couldn't understand it. You must know, Buffy, that I would never let anything happen to you. The house will not blow away, really."

He caressed her face in the dark, and she luxuriated in it. His scent enveloped her, and she trailed her hand from his bare shoulder to the denim waistband of his jeans, loving the smooth, lean feel of his shirtless back.

"I'm just scared silly of storms, Max. I always have been."

"Why? As a child, were you ever hurt in a storm?"

"No." Oh, this lying in Max's arms was like nothing she'd ever known before—like heaven. "I just remember waking up in the middle of the night. There was wind and lightning, and no one to turn to for comfort. I desperately wanted to run to my parents' bed and jump in between them. But I had no parents to sandwich me between them securely. It's really horrible to be alone, especially to be alone and a child. I'm all grown up now, Max. Able to cope with everything. But a storm will bring all that back to me, all that terrible insecurity."

He held her silently for a moment, not moving, barely breathing. And she wondered what he was thinking.

"Please don't think I'm a crazy, mixed-up kid, just because I go nuts in a storm. I've managed to overcome a lot of things in my life, and one day I'll conquer this phobia, too."

"I don't think any less of you," he whispered. "Your fears are not your fault. I have all the confidence in the world in you. I've seen you on the courts; I know you're strong."

Now that her hysteria was over and she had talked about the problem, he began to move away.

"No!" she cried. "Don't let me go. Let me stay with you tonight. I want to sleep in your arms. I've never felt so safe."

"Y-you don't know what you're asking."

She had the grace to blush ashamedly. "Just for one storm," she pleaded softly, "give me something to cling to."

"All right," he agreed roughly, dragging her arms from around his back. "Let me go put out the lantern where you left it on the floor. I'll be right back."

The bed sprung level. He was gone; he had left her in a great, lonely blackness. She got up too and groped her way down the hall to the dim light cast by the lantern. She found him in the kitchen, his back to her, looking like some great Hercules in the throes of a terrific battle. His arms were spread to either side of him on the counter. Every muscle in his back rippled tensely, his biceps bulged, his hands clenched into large tight fists.

"Max, what's wrong?"

He turned to face her, and his eyes went dark with passion. She had never before seen naked desire in a man's eyes, any more than she'd experienced a man's unselfish love. She was at a loss as to know how to cope.

"Max, you don't want to . . ." How did one come right out and say it? ". . . make love to me, do you?"

"No!" He turned around abruptly.

She walked toward him slowly, grappling with this new

problem. If he wanted to make love to her, what should she do? He was probably nearly engaged to Marlene. She was perhaps still engaged to Jeffrey. There would be no future in it, not even a nice lengthy affair; certainly not marriage. It would be a one-night thing. It would be wrong. But if he wanted it, she wasn't sure she could deny him. Some part of her didn't even want to deny him.

Her hand fluttered over the smooth wing of his back. "If you really want to . . ." she trembled.

"No! For God's sake, no! You're confused enough as it is. I'm trying to help you, not destroy you. You have to face Dunstan yet. You have to sort yourself out. I will not add to your confusion."

He had suffered a Gethsemane, reaching a moral decision that he knew was right. Only one thing remained—the cross.

"Come along." He opened his arms, and she melted into him. They walked over to the lantern, and he bent to turn it off. Then he lifted her into his arms and carried her to his bed, where he held her chastely, yet with a strange, loving sweetness, through the long night.

Upon opening her eyes, she knew it was morning, because there was a chink of light shining between a shutter and a window sash. The noise of motors had awakened her—a whirring drone that she didn't attempt to identify. As she began to come fully awake she turned her head softly and looked at Max. The room was still dark, but she could see him dimly. Max's arms had left her at some point during the early-morning hours and were now wrapped around him, straitjacket-style.

The sleep she'd slept last night had been deep, the only completely satisfying sleep she had ever known. The storm hadn't existed, nothing had, except the beautiful security of Max.

What a fine-looking man he was. Even in repose, he had vitality and strength. His mouth opened slightly and he gave a little sigh, then resumed a kind of irregular breathing, which indicated he might be deep in his own private dreams.

An unexpected ache clutched at her heart; it was a deep need to know every molecule of this man. Was this love—this compulsion to get within a man and tickle him from the inside out?

She moved toward him, the satin of her gown whispering against his folded arms. His hands slid into the material and lifted the soft swell of her breasts. He stirred and moaned negatively, but his hands had a will of their own.

She brought her lips into trembling contact with his, and he bit into her mouth like a hungry animal. His hands pulled at her and caressed her passionately, now on satin, now on silky skin.

She didn't know how to respond. She didn't know the ways women were supposed to make love back. But she wanted to learn. And Max was so adept at teaching, even while asleep.

She unzipped the front of her dress and shrugged it off her shoulders. His hands found the new skin, and his head bent to kiss it hungrily. She was lost in a fire, not knowing what she was doing and not really caring.

Suddenly the sound of a door slamming shot through the air, and she heard an amused, throaty voice say, "Well, well, Max. What *are* you up to?" The tall, slender woman slinked into the room and peered at Buffy, who lay in a pool of frozen shock. "And with a mere child."

Max opened his eyes, saw where he was, and breathed a barely audible, "My God." He swiftly attacked Buffy's bareness with deftly zippered white satin and remarked to Marlene coolly, "I didn't hear your plane."

"Obviously, darling," she cooed sarcastically.

"Is your father here, too?"

"Yes. We flew in together. Daddy dear wanted to make sure his paradise didn't blow away in the storm. Really, darling, you must get this little piece out of your bed, posthaste, you know how straight dear old Daddy is."

Buffy was already calling herself a couple of choice names for putting herself in this position and for enticing a poor, defenseless sleeping man into making love to her. He'd already told her last night he wasn't interested.

131

"Marlene is right." He got out of the bed and pulled her to her feet. "Go out the back way, Buffy. We musn't let Pons see you in my room." He pulled her through his bathroom to his private back door.

"What a little mite," Marlene commented loudly. "And what was her name? Buffy? How cute. But too young, Max. Just an infant."

In Buffy's muddled state of mind one thing stood out quite clearly: she had, in a few brief moments, developed a strong, and probably undying, hatred for Marlene.

She turned at the door and blurted out in shame and contrition, "Oh, Max, I'm so sorry." Boy, she had really messed things up good between Max and this creature Marlene. And for bringing more trouble on him she was genuinely sorry.

"It's quite all right, really." He smiled.

She opened the door and started to leave. Cool wind whipped her gown and tousled her curls.

He grasped her tiny wrist. "Buffy," he said suddenly, "I didn't mean to . . ." He paused, passing a hand through his hair. "I'm afraid I was dreaming; I hope I didn't get too out of hand with you."

"Oh, no, Max." Poor man—he thought it was all his fault. "You were a gentleman, really. There was only that little bit Marlene saw."

"Good," he whispered. His gray gaze warmed over her huge amber eyes and scarlet cheeks, and he smiled drolly, as if he were poking fun at himself.

"I'll see you later, Max. I hope you can explain all this to Marlene." She really doubted that he could, the evidence had been too damning. Marlene would think it was the morning after.

"We'll play some tennis later, perhaps." He drew her close, teasing her as only Max could. "You do make an enchanting bedfellow."

She blushed furiously. "I'm a shameless hussy and a tease."

"So true, but enchantingly innocent, nonetheless."

"Thank you for being there when I needed someone," she said sincerely.

"You're quite welcome, indeed. Now run along, it's still damp, and I don't want you catching cold in that flimsy thing you've got on."

She waved, held her long dress up to keep it from catching debris left by the storm, and skirted around a badly mangled bougainvillea toward her own back door.

She stopped, however, on the patio, then walked over to the cliffside to stare down at the beach, which was now littered with the wreckage and carnage of the storm—palm fronds, driftwood, black seaweed dredged up from the very bowels of the ocean.

The wind, now temperate, played with her dress and her hair. It was difficult to believe that just a few hours ago it had been a raging beast. How capricious weather was. How capricious was life. She stood motionless like the prow on a ship and fearfully wondered where her impulsive love play with Max would have led if Marlene hadn't interrupted.

"By Jove!" came a distinctly British exclamation from behind her.

She turned to see a rather cherubic face sitting, without benefit of a neck, atop a portly body. A fringe of silver hair ringed his shiny bald dome like a badly slipped halo. A pair of lively blue eyes twinkled at her in wicked glee.

"It can't be! But it is!" He advanced toward her mischievously. "A tiny golden Aphrodite set down on our poor, storm-swept island by repentant gods."

Mirthful laughter gurgled up into her throat and burst from between her lips. She had never been called a love goddess, and in view of the disastrous state of her love life, she found the title outrageously funny.

Holding out her hand in a naturally friendly greeting, she laughed. "You've got to be Lord Ponsonby."

He gallantly bowed over the proffered hand. "Not only is the child beautiful, but she's quick."

Buffy laughed again. "I've been dying to meet you."

His blue eyes twinkled at her as he confessed gravely,

133

"Fancy that. A young thing like you dying to meet me. You've quite captured my heart."

She giggled and wrinkled her nose at him in typical Buffyish charm. She liked him—deciding this as suddenly and as irrevocably as she had determined to dislike his daughter.

CHAPTER 8

Late afternoon found Buffy on the beach, scavenging for driftwood and seashells. The weather was calm and beautiful, the only signs of the hurricane being the unusual debris strewn all over the beach. She'd already found two huge horse conch shells, a king conch, and an interesting piece of gnarled driftwood.

Myaka, Ponsonby, and Max were spending the day divesting the house of its shutters and sawing up the huge fallen oak tree into firewood for the massive stone fireplace in Ponsonby's living room. She could hear the whir of the chain saw even now as she ambled the beach.

Where Marlene was she didn't know or care. Buffy had escaped to the beach right after lunch, an uncomfortable affair during which the sable-haired Marlene had fawned all over Max in an effusive way, which had set Buffy's teeth on edge. The jet-set beauty was obviously quite ready to forgive Max for any real or imaginary indiscretions he'd committed with Buffy that morning.

She had treated Buffy with amicable scorn all during the meal, as one would an unwelcome puppy that had suddenly been dropped on one's doorstep. Her mask of politeness slipped badly a few times when she shot Buffy scorching undercover looks that would have withered the hardiest person.

Buffy, a fighter by nature, had met fire with fire. She hoped to let Marlene know, by her bold amber blazes of silence, that she wasn't dealing with some delicate English pansy but a fiery-tempered American girl who had come up the hard way.

Temperamentally she kicked mushy seaweed out of her way as she traveled the beach. She didn't care if Marlene was Max's paramour, she would not cower under to a rich, overindulged, supercilious snob who'd had everything handed to her on a silver platter.

Not only did Marlene have everything material that a woman could want, she was in possession of the one thing Buffy had always coveted—a loving, doting parent. Ponsonby, for all his jovial play and ridiculous antics, was a peach. And Marlene treated him like an overstuffed puppet. The way she ordered her father around galled Buffy almost beyond endurance. And the way she treated Loa was worse. She had complained about everything the capable black woman brought to the table, until Buffy had wanted to lift her plate and smash the lovely food into Marlene's lovely face.

She looked around the cluttered beach wanly. Ponsonby's Island had suddenly become like someplace east of Eden. It was no longer a paradise—and not just because it had been visited by a hurricane.

She trudged up the cliffside to the house, depositing her treasures on a warm patio slab to dry in the sun. Max came toward her with Marlene firmly leeched into his arm.

"How about that game of tennis you promised me?" he asked mildly while strolling up to her. "The courts are quite dry. Marlene and I just inspected them."

Buffy cast a glance at the gorgeous, slick-haired Marlene and saw glittering in the coal-black eyes a threat that seemed to say, "Stay away; he's mine."

Buffy wrinkled her nose at Max as cutely as possible and grinned broadly. "I'd love to," she said without a moment's hesitation.

Marlene wiped an expression of sheer hatred off her face just before Max turned to her. "You and Pons come out and watch us play. Buffy is an ace at tennis, a real champion. Pons has already expressed the desire to watch her in action."

"Wouldn't miss it for the world," Marlene cooed up at

him in a voice that would melt sugar. "Daddy and I will meet you both at the courts in twenty minutes."

Max extracted his arm from her serpentine grasp and excused himself. After he'd disappeared through the glass sliding doors, she turned to Buffy and remarked in polite sarcasm, "Max is quite taken by your expertise in tennis. He's talked of little else since we arrived. What a pity he finds you so disappointing in other more vital areas." She flicked an imaginary dust particle off the low-cut halter top she was wearing, which revealed all too clearly that her own vital areas were very adequate.

Buffy stiffened. She didn't need Marlene to let her know that she didn't have the equipment to interest a man like Max. Marlene was beautiful, from the top of her sleek pageboy to the tips of her painted toenails, and all the ample curves in between. There was no contest to it.

Marlene laughed throatily and circled around Buffy like a feline stalking prey. "He told me nothing has happened between you two. Over a week on this island together, and nothing has happened! That should indicate something."

"It's none of your damned business," Buffy said, disgusted beyond further expression.

"Oh, but it is! The pure chemical inconsistency of it interests me no end. You see, I know Max Shepherd quite well." She shot Buffy a look that indicated how much of an understatement this was. "We have been, shall we say, close. He is an animal of great virility." Marlene hooded her eyes as if moments of sublime ecstasy were brought to her remembrance. "That is why I was prepared to forgive him his indulgences with you, if it were necessary. We must be broad-minded, after all, in this day and time. All of Max's women friends are aware of that."

"What the hell are you talking about?" Buffy had lapsed back into her old, colorful way of expressing herself, and her temper pulled against its restraints like a mettlesome racehorse.

"Chemistry, darling." Marlene smiled venomously. "It's quite unnatural that Max has not made love to you heretofore. It is, in fact, an indictment against your womanhood." She passed a contemptuous glance over Buffy's girlishly petite figure, sneering slightly at the blond wind-blown curls, seeming to understand why Max's natural inclinations had not found expression. "Poor Max. When it gets out that he's had a girl on this island for a whole week and nothing has happened, it may wreck his reputation. He is known as the Casanova of the jet set, you know."

"Liar!" Buffy hissed. "Max is a perfect gentleman. He is too honorable to be a womanizer."

Marlene guffawed most unattractively. "How naive you are! There are half a dozen women who would give their diamond necklaces to have been in your position for the past week, and half a dozen more who have already been there, including myself." She looked up at the sky rapturously. "Oh, when I think of our stolen vacation in Majorca!"

"It's nothing to brag about," Buffy spat scornfully, yet breathlessly, as if she were suffering from a jagged knife wound.

"Why not?" Marlene purred, apparently contented for the moment that she was doing some real damage to Buffy's ego. "Max is a tempting hunk of manflesh, you have to admit." She held out a beautifully manicured hand and examined lovely fire-engine-red claws nonchalantly. "And he doesn't mind showing his full virility with a real woman. But that's where you're sadly lacking, isn't it. Which leaves, shall we say, a clear field of play for me."

"Oh, you're too gross for words," Buffy choked, and ran to her room.

Not twenty minutes later the revulsion and anger she felt at hearing about Max's nefarious love life was expressed on the courts in the form of trying to murder a tiny, fuzzy gray ball.

She'd figured that a man as good-looking as Max wouldn't be a celibate priest at the age of thirty-three, but he hadn't seemed the type who would conquer women for the sport of it. That she couldn't hold a candle to the women he was accustomed to did not surprise her; but this revelation concerning his personal life did, painfully.

She won the first set and he ran to the net, laughing, his dark, silky head wet with perspiration. "What demon has got you today? You're killing me."

"Nothing personal, Max," she panted. How could she blame him, after all, for merely being a man? Women undoubtedly fell at his feet. "Just a lot of pent-up energy, I guess." She had, herself, last night. It wasn't his fault that he didn't find her appealing.

Marlene stared at her stonily from the sidelines, and Lord Ponsonby gave her a high sign as she took her stance behind the service line.

The ball whizzed back and forth as if jet propelled. Max managed to win a set, but she won the next two, her angry frenzy finally having spent itself.

Ponsonby yelled, "Bravo," from the sidelines; Max bounded across the net and whirled her around in his arms. "You're fantastic." He seemed overjoyed that she'd beaten him by using some of the very techniques he'd taught her.

Ponsonby approached her, a grin splitting his plump, cherubic face. "Wimbledon material if I ever saw it! You whipped Max soundly, my child. Good show!"

"Oh, let's do get out of this beastly heat, Daddy," Marlene complained. She took off her exotic sunshades and delicately wiped the bridge of her nose.

The portly Lord Ponsonby allowed his daughter to bulldoze him toward the house, but not before turning and commenting, "She plays like a dynamo, that one. If you don't take her to Wimbledon, Max, I shall."

Buffy, warmed and pleased under his praise, wiped her face with a hand towel and remarked, "Now there's a man with a lot of faith in me."

"I have faith in you," Max said, hugging her with a sweaty arm. "And when the time comes for you to go to Wimbledon, I claim the honor of taking you there." He smiled down at her, piercing her with his unfathomable gray eyes.

139

Because he was teasing, she responded lightly, "And I would gladly let you."

"Would you?" he softened.

"Yes, but I doubt if Jeffrey would approve. I might be Mrs. Dunstan by then."

His arm froze, and he withdrew it stiffly. His face darkened like a thundercloud. "You're not ready to get married. I thought we had established that fact."

"I don't consider you an authority on the subject of marriage," she said tightly, remembering what Marlene had told her.

"It doesn't take an authority to see that you are not mature enough to handle marriage. It's a forever proposition, you know." He flipped his towel impatiently over his shoulder and steered her toward the house.

He had a lot of nerve, talking about forever arrangements. All his past talk about the sublime state of true love was a lot of ballyhoo. All that insistence on the reality of lasting romance was pure hypocrisy.

"What's good for the gander is good for the goose," she said snootily, twisting a meaningless phrase into further meaninglessness.

"What a frightfully stupid thing to say." His hand bit into her arm, and she pulled away contemptuously.

"You're always putting me down, aren't you? Always calling me dumb."

Their steps had grown quick and angry as they walked through the shady pine grove to Ponsonby's house. "No!" He twirled her around to face him. "I just want you to break it off with Dunstan when you get back, Buffy." There was a strained earnestness in his voice, which completely eluded her. "He's not for you, believe me."

"How can you know that? You've never met him." She put her hands on his damp shirt, feeling the solid strength underneath and wondering why this man, inaccessible as heaven itself, had such a strange effect on her. "Oh, Max. Let's not fuss. It hurts me when you're angry."

"Oh, Buffy, Buffy," he whispered tormentedly. "How

can I make you understand without rushing over you like a freight train?"

"Understand what?"

He shook his head. "Time. Time is what you need." And this pronouncement made no sense at all to her.

For dinner that evening, Loa presented a bountiful platter of grouper steaks broiled to perfection in garlic butter. Buffy ate with pleasure, savoring the mild, flaky white meat. The vegetables served with the fish were steamed and remained crisp, just the way she liked them.

Marlene, on the other hand, picked at her food and wouldn't touch the beautiful cherries jubilee dessert. Buffy suspected Marlene, being so adapted to a life of inactivity, had to keep a tight rein on her appetite, or all her perfect voluptuousness would run quickly to fat. That was a nice thought: Marlene, fat. Buffy giggled into her wine.

After coffee Lord Ponsonby suggested that he and Max retire to the study to talk business. He was anxious to hear all about the new project on Caicos. Ambling down the hall toward the study, he offered Max a cigar and slapped him on the back, making a comment that he would have to buy a yacht so that he could visit the new resort after it was built. Then he boomed a hearty laugh at his joke.

Marlene looked after Max's receding back hungrily. "Wretched business," she murmured, "this dividing of the sexes after dinner. I do wish dear old Daddy would come out of the dark ages a bit."

"Why do you speak of your father in terms of such disrespect?" Buffy snapped. "You don't know how lucky you are."

"Look, Little Miss All-American Tennis Star, I don't need you to correct me on the proper way to conduct myself toward my father, or anyone else, for that matter." Claws were unsheathed, hatred unveiled.

"You certainly do need someone to correct you," Buffy menaced. "You're the most spoiled, selfish, and thoroughly unlikable individual I've ever met up with." Far be it from Buffy to be unwilling to trade insult for insult.

"You're a clever little gold digger for all your pretended

innocence." Marlene glittered hatefully. "It's obvious you're trying to ingratiate yourself with my father."

"I like your father!" Buffy hissed across the lace tablecloth, highly incensed by this suggestion that she was trying to get into Lord Ponsonby's good graces because he was wealthy. "It's just beyond me how such a nice man could have ever fathered something like you."

Marlene's eyes narrowed to two black slits, and bright patches of anger flamed to her creamy cheeks. "We have to watch out for little nobodies like you all the time," she snarled. "We'd have scores of parasites crawling about the place if we weren't careful. Might I remind you that you've been here for several days, living off our bounty. Uninvited."

"You would be the type to bring that up. Never mind that Max and I had to either land here or crash into the ocean. And I'll have you know I'm not a nobody. I'm well known in my profession. I have money in the bank—money I've sweated to earn, which is more than I can say for you."

"Bully!" the cold-eyed sophisticate burst out.

An icy silence settled between them as Loa came in to take the dishes away. Buffy's gaze shifted from Marlene's hypnotic stare to Loa's fearful expression, and she knew the servant had heard all. But any warning message Loa was trying to send through the silent, tense atmosphere went completely unnoticed, for Buffy, in all her tiger-gold glory, was prepared to rise to any kind of slanging match Marlene wanted to have.

"Why, Miss Marlene," Loa gulped meekly, intending in her gentle, simplistic way to soothe the air, "you didn't touch your dessert."

"Take that rubbish away," she ordered Loa rudely, nearly shoving it off the table. "It was awful. I don't know why Daddy keeps you on."

This was too spiteful, too malicious, too cruel to a gentle woman whose only desire in life was to please. Buffy rose her full five-foot-two-inch height to a monument of indignant fury, spluttering virtriolically, "Don't you dare talk to her like that. Don't you dare treat her like a slave."

Marlene rose too, her blackly sheathed presence towering considerably over her opponent, her angry eyes shooting daggers across the table.

Loa gave a little cry of protest. "Please, Miss Buffy. "It's all right." She had been about to add that she was used to such treatment when Marlene's shrill words cut her off:

"How dare you insult me in front of a servant!"

"How dare you insult one of my friends. Don't ever do it again," Buffy issued in deadly ultimatum, "or you will be sorry."

Loa was nearly sobbing now, dumbly looking from one adversary to the other.

The appalling encounter went from the low degree of mere incivility to the pit of savagery when Marlene whispered, "Bitch!"

Buffy, never one to be outdone at name-calling, countered with a clear and sibilant, "Pig!"

"Buffy!" Max's vibrant, forceful voice cut between them like a rapier. "Go to your room."

Max was livid. Ponsonby was amused. Loa flapped her apron and escaped to the kitchen. Marlene, who had been at the point of leaping at Buffy's throat, purred contentedly—she had come off the injured party. Max had apparently only heard Buffy's last, and very unladylike, attack.

"You don't understand," the now tearful Buffy tried to explain. "She—"

"Go to your room!" he thundered. And she fled.

The next morning, she waited in her room until she was reasonably sure everyone had eaten breakfast. She advanced into the living room furtively and, not hearing the sound of human activity within the house, peeked through velvet draperies to scout out the pool area.

There were Max and Marlene, arm in arm, dressed in

bathing suits, heading for the path on the cliff that led to the narrow, secluded beach below.

Marlene was talking to Max coquettishly, hugging his arm to her ample bosom the whole time, making her availability as blatant as possible.

She's probably telling him her version of what happened last night, Buffy thought. She saw Max look down at Marlene and laugh at something she said. He affectionately patted her hand, which was wrapped firmly around his bicep.

Oh, yes, Marlene would be poking a good deal of sophisticated fun at how a scrappy little ruffian had the audacity to verbally attack a well-bred woman of the world.

She watched them descend into the air in front of the cliff. Max's dark windblown hair was the last thing to disappear, leaving only a serene horizon of cliff and sky.

Well, that was that. I wouldn't be many moments before he would be lost in her generous embrace. And Buffy realized painfully that she had done a great deal toward driving him there.

A short, frustrated breath full of all sorts of unspoken imprecations burst from her mouth. She turned in miserable anger to find Lord Ponsonby watching her shrewdly.

"I-I was just checking the weather," she explained uncomfortably. He would have no way of knowing what she had really been watching and how wretched it made her feel.

"A sunny eighty degrees. Wind out of the southwest, five miles per hour. Lovely," he reported to her. He held out a hand and motioned her to the dining room. "Come along and have some breakfast, you must be famished."

There was a sincere kindness beneath the man's courtesy, which touched her deeply, for she didn't deserve it after calling his daughter such a terrible name while he was within earshot.

Sitting down at the table, she spread her napkin over her knees and repented. "I'm sorry," she blurted out. "I feel terrible about what you heard me call your daughter last night. It must have shocked you deeply."

144

He twinkled bluely. "My dear child, at my age, one is well beyond shock. I jolly well know my own daughter. I daresay she contributed her fair share to the quarrel."

"Just the same, please forgive me."

"No need to apologize at all. Max made all your apologies for you this morning. Marlene told Max she forgave you and kissed him soundly." Again he seemed to be watching her closely.

She blanched at this news. The mental picture of Marlene attached to Max's lips seared her with despair. Unbidden tears brimmed her eyes. "Isn't that nice," she managed to choke.

Ponsonby smiled secretly and mumbled incoherently, "This is most interesting." He pushed through the kitchen door, calling, "Fix this child some breakfast, Loa."

"Already have, Boss." Loa came through the swinging door, carrying a tray of coffee and food.

Buffy sat alone at the huge dining table and ate what she could. A painful vision ghosted her mind—Marlene and Max in a lover's embrace. That was what was going on right now down on the secluded beach. She was sure of it. And with a woman like Marlene, things could proceed to only one conclusion—the act itself.

She clutched her coffee cup in front of her and tried to bring a curtain down against that picture. But it flashed across her brain grotesquely like an old-time movie reel. Her stomach roiled, and she groaned.

Oh, God, she realized, I'm acting like the wife who has caught her husband being unfaithful. She tried to pull herself together. I don't have any claim on Max, she reasoned. I'm merely a piece of troublesome baggage to him. He and Marlene have been lovers. There's no reason why he shouldn't resume that relationship with her again, since she is so willing. I mustn't be upset, I mustn't be upset.

She continued to hold the cup in a death grip as she marched into the kitchen with it.

"More coffee, Miss Buffy?" Loa asked. "I could have brought it to you."

"No, no." She set the cup down distractedly. "Just

needing some company. Do you mind if I hang around a while and watch you work?" She walked around the kitchen, touching counters and appliances, movement being her only answer to worry and pain.

"Sure." Loa smiled at her in near adoration. Gratitude was written all over her smooth, black face. "Thank you for calling me friend last night, Miss Buffy. Thank you for trying to help me. But you mustn't again. You stay away from that Marlene. She pretty damn tough."

"Well, I'm pretty damn tough, too," Buffy said stoutly. "And if she ever talks ugly to you again, she'll find out just how tough."

"She mean, Miss Buffy. You stay away from her. She used to tear her dolls to pieces just for fun. She love to destroy things. Always has."

"She'd better not try that with me. I'm no defenseless doll. She may be bigger than I am, but I'm ten times quicker." Although being a natural competitor and very physical, Buffy had never wanted to come into hand-to-hand combat with anyone before—that is, until now. "I don't see what Max sees in her," she muttered fiercely.

"Mr. Shepherd don't see anything in her." Loa smiled knowingly. "Mr. Shepherd, he love you. He may get mad, but he love you right on."

Buffy looked up to the ceiling. Here we go round the mulberry bush again, she thought. Rather than argue the point with her good friend, she told Loa she would see her later and sauntered off to her room.

A half hour later she was on the court with a can of balls, a racket, and a large plywood shutter that she'd dragged onto the playing surface from the place nearby where Myaka and Max had stacked them temporarily. If Max wanted to go cavorting on the beach with Marlene, she'd play tennis alone.

She leaned the plywood against the net and began methodically practicing every new technique Max had taught her until she had them down pat. The ball always hit where she wanted it to and bounced back dependably. It was lonely, this solitary play, but satisfying.

146

She left the court played out, having learned nothing at all except how to put a little round object precisely where she aimed it against an immobile target—a small measure of control in an infinitely uncontrollable world.

After showering she wrapped in her terry-cloth robe and lay down for a while. She dozed, but was awakened by Max's attractive laughter and muted voices. Max must be back from his rendezvous in the sand with Marlene, she thought. She flung her arm over her eyes and tried to blot everything out.

A little while later there was a soft rap at the door. Loa poked her head in, and Buffy motioned her to enter.

"What is it, Loa?" she asked.

"I bring you something." She approached the bed shyly with a piece of silky material draped over her arms. It was a wildly patterned piece of orange, fuchsia, pink, and cream flowers. She laid the beautiful material on the bed and placed a half-opened perfect hibiscus beside it. "A present to my friend."

"Oh, it's the most gorgeous piece of material I've ever seen! I'll have a dress made of it when I get home."

"It already a dress," Loa beamed. "You wear. Boss order barbecue on patio for dinner. You wear this, you look very pretty. I buy it in Freeport last year, but never wear. I want you to have."

Buffy looked at the exotic yet fragile piece of material that Loa claimed was a dress and murmured, "Thank you."

Loa laughed delightedly. "Up! Get up, Miss Buffy. I show you how to put it on."

"But I don't have any underclothes on," she protested as Loa pulled her to her feet.

"Not necessary." She stripped the robe off Buffy and quick as a wink wound her in the soft material, pulling ends through slotted sides and tying them securely under young, upthrust breasts.

Buffy hadn't time to be embarrassed over her brief moments of nudity, and Loa was certainly nowhere near

147

being embarrassed. On the contrary, she seemed infinitely pleased by the whole process.

"But, Loa," she spluttered, "I don't even have a pair of panties on under this."

"No need. Panties show through," Loa protested. "Your young, perfect skin better," she explained. Moving Buffy over to stand her before the mirror, she said proudly, "See how pretty."

The dress had all the effect of an expensive original—something a movie star would spend hundreds of dollars on just to lounge about the pool in. There were no straps at all and a long skirt, which Loa, by some miracle, had wound so deftly as to slit up one leg to reveal Buffy's firm, golden thigh.

Panty lines *would* show through, she thought. Even a tiny dimple would, if she had one. As it was, what she did have was all too clearly defined—and looked pretty good, she had to admit.

But she couldn't wear the dress. It was scandalous. It went against her natural modesty and her strict moral upbringing. She would wear the pink chiffon. Chiffon at a barbecue? No, she would wear her floral Qiana dress. But how to tell Loa without hurting her feelings?

"That Marlene, she always wear black," Loa said, admiring Buffy's image in the mirror. "Since the age of sixteen, she wear black. She say it soph—sophis—" she stumbled.

"Sophisticated," Buffy supplied.

"Yes." Loa humphed and arranged the hibiscus in the blond curls above Buffy's ear. "You wear this to dinner. You come out looking like a little love flower. Marlene, she wear black and look like evil. You make her look sick."

Now, there was a thought—making Marlene look sick. Could it be done? Did she have the nerve to try? She saw in the mirror her young maidenly nipples imprinted clearly, as was the soft fullness around them. She turned, and the dents in her small buttocks were marked clearly and softly.

Oh, what the heck! Her appearance couldn't corrupt anyone. Ponsonby was too old. And Max didn't care.

She walked from the mirror confidently, her mind made up. And as she did, every line of her body moved supplely with promises of warm womanliness.

Loa went to the door, giving Buffy one last look. They exchanged smiles, and Buffy said, "Thanks, Loa."

"Thank you, Miss Buffy." She was infinitely satisfied with her piece of work that afternoon. It paid a little for all the rudeness she had suffered at Marlene's hands.

Buffy did her face, finishing by brushing on a dripping petal-pink lipstick. Then she walked to the patio impulsively for fear that by lingering in her room she would change her mind about wearing the outrageous dress.

The smoky tang of charcoal assailed her nostrils as she opened the sliding glass doors. Marlene sat at a patio table, nursing a cocktail. Fulfilling Loa's prediction, she wore black, a satin backless jump suit, which fit like a seal's skin. She took in Buffy's appearance at a single sweeping glance, and her lips curled maliciously.

Buffy wound her way around patio furniture toward Max and Ponsonby, who were standing over a huge brick barbecue pit, both looking at her agog.

"Hi," she greeted brightly, then bent over the grill to inhale the tantalizing aroma of sizzling meat. "Mmm. I just love a barbecue."

Ponsonby twinkled at her gnomishly as if there were a marvelous joke underway. "My my, but don't you look enchanting." He turned to Max, chuckling lowly, his keen blue eyes not missing a particle of Max's reaction. "Quite fetching, isn't she, dear boy?"

Silver eyes moltenly traveled over every inch of her body, then rested on moist, pink lips and held there as his arm silently snaked out to grasp a drink beside the pit. The muscles in his throat worked convulsively as he downed it.

Marlene slithered into the picture, demurely demanding, "Please freshen my drink, Max." He took her glass absently, still staring down at a vision of gold and blond and

149

everything hinted at under a pattern of wild colors. "Max!" she said sharply. "My drink!"

"Yes, of course," he murmured vacantly before departing to a nearby portable bar.

Buffy noted with satisfaction that Marlene looked a bit white around the gills and hoped fervently that she'd been responsible for some of her discomfiture.

Lord Ponsonby seemed enormously amused. "Oh, the delicious circumstances life visits upon us," he chortled. "The older I get, the more I'm inclined to agree with my esteemable fellow countryman, Shakespeare: 'Life is but a stage.'"

"What drivel!" Marlene exploded. "Why do you insist upon finding fun in everything?"

Buffy bristled at Marlene's disrespect of her father and retreated to a nearby lounge chair as Ponsonby shrugged and turned back to the steaks.

Marlene undulated over to Buffy and settled herself in a chair near her. Putting on a sweet mask, she said, "Max tells me you're engaged to a fellow in the States."

"That's debatable," Buffy replied. "I didn't show up for the wedding. He may have called the whole thing off permanently, for all I know."

"Is that why you're not wearing his ring?"

"Jeffrey was going to give me a diamond after the wedding."

"How odd." Marlene fingered a diamond earring fondly.

Buffy thought those chandeliers too extravagant to wear to a barbecue, but she supposed the rich couldn't resist displaying their wealth. "It's not odd at all," she countered. "We kept the engagement a secret, because Jeffrey dislikes publicity of any kind concerning his personal life. He knew the press would make a big show of the marriage. He's a professional tennis player, too."

"I see," Marlene flickered with interest.

"We athletes like publicity only when it concerns our abilities. That's why all professionals try so hard to avoid scandal," Buffy explained. "We have to walk a narrow line. The public expects us to behave circumspectly and

150

live clean lives. Of course, I wouldn't have minded our engagement being common knowledge. I didn't see how reporters could twist it into anything it wasn't. But Jeffrey insisted we release a quiet statement to the papers after the wedding. He is almost fanatical about keeping his personal life private."

"Yes, why take chances?" Marlene purred like the cat swallowing the proverbial canary. "With so much at stake."

Max approached with her drink and handed one to Buffy. "It's only Coke with a dash of rum," he informed her, sitting on the foot of her lounge chair. "I know you don't like to drink."

"Thanks, Max." She smiled at him guilelessly.

"Buffy has been telling me all about her fiancé," Marlene said to him.

"Oh, yes, Dunstan." He looked into his own drink and frowned.

"Isn't it marvelous to be young and so much in love?"

Max brooded over his drink and seethed volcanically.

Buffy wriggled back into the lounge chair, amazed at Marlene's blundering. Didn't she know that Max disapproved heartily of her and Jeffrey's engagement? She decided to sit silently and watch Marlene hang herself.

"They're not in love," Max spoke curtly.

"Oh, but of course they are," she argued.

Ponsonby whistled tunelessly from afar off; the air around them was charged with tension. "Stay out of it," Max ordered. "You don't know Buffy as I do."

The subject at hand bit her lip delightedly. They were arguing over her—it was too good to be true.

"I guess I know a woman in love when I see one," Marlene spoke venomously.

Buffy thought Marlene was taking a bit too much for granted here and started to protest.

"Leave it alone," Max rasped out, getting up angrily to stride over to help Ponsonby with the steaks.

Loa wheeled out a trolley laden with salads. She treaded

softly around the edge of the pool to where Buffy had gotten up to meet her.

"I make your favorite yogurt and fruit salad, Miss Buffy," she whispered.

Marlene, now at breaking point, shaded her eyes from the sun's glare on the pool and snarled, "We don't need a rundown on the menu, Loa. Your job is merely to prepare the food and serve it. And may I remind you that you work for me, not this little chit."

Buffy turned on Marlene, fiercely whispering, "You apologize to her immediately. She doesn't deserve such treatment."

Marlene uncoiled out of her chair and faced Buffy squarely, still squinting from the brilliant blue of the pool. "I don't apologize to anyone," she menaced, "least of all to a servant."

"Well, you will this time."

"How dare you!" Marlene, choking with bitter bile and frustration, completely lost control and lunged at Buffy with both hands.

It all happened so fast that Max only caught the tail end of it—the part where Buffy sidestepped adroitly, whisked in behind Marlene, at the same time putting a petite size five foot in her black backside, and shoved forcefully. Marlene screamed, arms and legs awry, and did a magnificent belly flop into the pool.

CHAPTER 9

Buffy closed her eyes in panic. *Oh, I don't believe I did that. I didn't.* She opened her eyes, and the sight of a thoroughly sopped Marlene thrashing in the sparkling water assured her that indeed she had. It had been a reflex action more than anything else, for she was a creature trained to respond with physical quickness on the courts. *Max will kill me for this,* she doomed herself.

Ponsonby was extending a helping hand to his daughter, who was struggling up the ladder, her black jump suit sleekly wet, her pageboy hair plastered to her head like a seal's cap, all sorts of unintelligible threats coming from her mouth.

Suddenly Max had Buffy under the elbow and was marching her practically on her tippy-toes all the way to her room. And he didn't release this high-handed grasp until after he'd kicked her door shut and twirled her around to face him.

"You little idiot!" he raged. "Don't you know the first thing about how to behave yourself?"

Although she knew that it was not Marlene Ponsonby, but Buffy Vallentine, who was sunk, she didn't care. She was in a sudden fury that Max was the type of man who found a woman like Marlene attractive.

"She deserved it," Buffy blazed defiantly. "I'm only sorry I didn't have time to tie a lead weight to her foot before I kicked her in."

He released her abruptly and did a few angry paces about the room, then ran a hand through his fine silky hair exasperatedly. "Damn it, Buffy. You can't keep on

153

putting Marlene in these rages. Why can't you go on your merry way and pay no attention to her? You don't have to like her, just be polite to her. How do you think all this catfighting makes Pons feel? You come along and accept his hospitality—eat his food, use his home—then kick his daughter into the pool. It's barbaric."

"Oh!" she mocked sarcastically, placing one hand on her hip, which she slung out to one side and jiggled angrily. "Bad manners! Mustn't have bad manners. It's a no-no for me to give Marlene a swift honest kick for all the world to see, but perfectly all right for you to have an illicit affair with her behind her father's back. You're a damned hypocrite," she spat.

He stopped his pacing and pinned her down with a look of pure astonishment. "Would you mind explaining that accusation, please?" he asked in a voice undertoned with ice. "I'm not sure I understood you correctly."

"Certainly! I know all about you—your reputation with women. I know that you and Marlene were once lovers." Her voice rose to an hysterical pitch. "I know that you two went down to the beach together this morning. And please don't say it was to collect shells. And here I thought you were a proper English gentleman," she mocked. "Hasn't anyone ever told you that it's bad manners to accept a man's hospitality while at the same time dallying with his daughter?"

Her voice began to die out as his eyes grew as coldly gray as the Arctic Ocean. She continued to speak, but weakly. "Obviously people like you live by some sort of double standard. Laws of common decency don't apply to you . . . just everyone else. You're rich, titled—you don't have to be really respectable as long as the facade of it is there. Well, you can have Marlene." She was whispering now. "You two make a terrific couple. . . ." And her voice trailed off into an abyss of misery—words she would never be able to recall.

"Have you quite finished?" His tone cut like ice. She nodded and swallowed thickly.

He advanced toward her and trickles of fear slithered

154

up and down her spine. He grabbed her tiny blond head and crushed her curls in massive fists. She drew in a quick breath from the pain of it.

"You believe it," he whispered savagely, drawing her face close to his. A look of cold fury quickly replaced the intense agony that had fleeted across his face. "You actually believe it."

"Marlene told me, herself." She tried to twist free of his hold, but his hands clenched tighter. She had a wild premonition that he was on the verge of doing something really violent to her.

"After everything—all the giving, not asking for anything in return—you can believe something like that? It has all been for nothing?"

His hands released her hair, and he drew her into a male body seared with the heat of emotion. By now her head was throbbing, and all her bones cried out against the fierceness of his embrace.

"It would give me a great deal of pleasure to rip you out of this flimsy tissue-paper wrapping you've got on and rape you thoroughly," he breathed thickly into her ear. "It's what you deserve." One of his hands held her back while the other slipped and clutched her small, boyish derriere, pulling that part of her into him with crushing savagery.

"Max." It was a high whimper.

"Shut up!" he slurred. "I've heard enough. Now you can listen while I tell you exactly what I would like to do to you. How I would like to finally lose control and plunder all the soft treasures you so wantonly flaunted in front of me today." She closed her eyes and swam in half-conscious blackness. "How I would love to rip into your virginity like a lusting animal, in too much of a heated passion to heed your cries of pain. I would brutally take everything a man wants and prove to you that I am the beast you think I am. Oh, the delight of it tempts me almost beyond endurance."

Suddenly he released her, and she fell back on the bed, taking in great, sobbing breaths. "Get your things together," he bit out. "I'm taking you off this island immediately." He strode to the door, but before departing, turned around to finish contemptuously, "I pity poor Dunstan if he's fool enough to marry you. You know nothing of love and giving, much less trust."

She sat in a stupor after he left, her glance finally falling to the floor. There something lay which she didn't immediately recognize. Bending to pick it up, she saw that it was what remained of the half-opened hibiscus she'd worn in her hair, now crushed and broken and weeping against her hand.

She barely had time to change into a modest pantsuit and pack her bags before Max came through her door and briskly bore them away, with a silent nod ordering her to follow.

He dropped the bags in front of the telephone and told her to call Jeffrey and tell him to meet her at the Miami airport in sixty minutes.

"Th-that's not necessary," she stammered. "I can take a taxi back to the apartment."

He lifted the receiver and thrust it into her hand. "I said call him," he ordered coldly. "I shall see you safely deposited in his arms before I leave you."

It wasn't easy to inform Jeffrey of her impending arrival in Miami, due to the static on the line and the tremors in her voice, but she finally managed to make him understand before dumbly hanging up.

Max grasped her elbow, hauled her out of her chair, picked up her bags, and nodded in the direction of the back door.

Loa stood over the kitchen sink, washing dishes. Beautiful barbecued steaks were heaped on a platter on the counter, untouched.

Buffy fell out of the line in which Max expected her to walk, moving over to touch Loa on the shoulder. Loa turned a red-eyed, tear-stained face to her, and Buffy nearly burst into tears herself.

"I've caused you trouble," she trembled. "Please forgive me."

"Miss Buffy, Miss Buffy," was all Loa could reply.

She heard an impatient noise from Max and marched back into line like a prisoner of war.

The colorful canopied golf cart moved jauntily through the late-afternoon glow of a dying sun. The beauties of the island paradise couldn't thrill her now as they had on her arrival, for she was in a private hell of her own making.

Ponsonby was at the plane along with Myaka, who regarded her with a silent, soulful expression.

Max lifted her into Ponsonby's plane with as little ceremony as he did the baggage. She knew she couldn't leave the island without expressing some apology to Lord Ponsonby for her behavior.

"I'm so sorry," she said, leaning toward him, barely under control.

Silver eyebrows, sporting more bush than seemed natural for such an otherwise hairless head, contracted into a frown—but it didn't seem like an angry frown. "Most unfortunate train of circumstances," he puzzled. "It didn't end up at all like I imagined it would." He turned to Max distressfully. "Really, Max, there's no need to whisk her off like this."

"I'll have your plane back tonight, Pons," Max cut in politely but firmly. "Thank you so much for being so generous to lend it to me."

He hoisted himself into the plane without any further comment, and within a remarkably short period of time, had it airborne.

She wanted to cry but wouldn't give in to it. She also wanted to tell him she was sorry for passing judgment on his personal life. After all, what went on between him and Marlene was none of her business. Just because she was miserable over it was no reason to lash out at him abusively. She remained, however, in a stupor of silence, not knowing how to talk, or even how to think.

Gray wisps of evening had set in when their plane taxied to a stop on the Miami runway. He hadn't uttered a word. Nor did he when he hauled her roughly to the concrete and pulled out her luggage.

157

Her shoes made sharp clicking sounds on the pavement as she hurried behind him toward the terminal.

"Max!" She gulped down a whole ocean of unshed tears. He didn't alter his stride. "Oh, Max, you can't leave me like this."

"There's nothing else to be done," he said curtly, opening glass doors and pushing her through. He dropped her bags on the cold terrazzo floor with a thud of finality and combed the poorly-lit terminal with eyes the color of steel.

"There's your young man." He nodded toward Jeffrey, who was approaching them, wearing a smile of welcome. "He seems pleased to have you back."

Jeffrey hugged her, and she responded with all the fervor of a rag doll. "Honey, you had us all worried sick," he said affectionately, holding her to his side as he stuck out a hand to Max. "Jeff Dunstan."

Max smiled tightly and shook the proffered hand. "Max Shepherd."

"Thank you for bringing her home."

"You're quite welcome."

Buffy felt as if she were going to become violently ill any moment.

"How can I repay you?"

"No need."

"But I feel like I should. You've gone to a lot of trouble, and fuel is expensive."

"Perhaps you would allow me to kiss the bride," Max suggested. "Since I won't be around when the wedding takes place."

"Sure." Jeffrey laughed, dropping his arm from Buffy's waist.

Oh, no, she groaned inwardly. Not this. Oh, god, not this. She locked her knees to keep them from completely collapsing and lifted her face to him.

His gray, impassive eyes held her transfixed for a moment that seemed to stretch into infinity. His hand rested on her neck, and his lips brushed across her cheek to her ear, enveloping her in his dizzying masculine scent and an aura of noble strength.

"Good-bye," he whispered.

No, she cried silently. Don't leave me. I love you. I can't make it without you.

But he was already heading toward the door, his broad wedge of a back held stiffly, his hands shoved deep into his pockets.

No! she screamed, and her brain reeled from the deafening silent roar of it. Don't go. I love you.

"Snap out of it, Buffy," Jeffrey urged as he grabbed her bags off the floor. "We have a helluva lot of talking to do, you and I."

He drove her to his parents' house, a plush sprawling affair located in Waterbrook Estates, designed and built by the best contractors in Florida. She talked as little as possible, still rocked by the blinding admission she'd just made to herself—she loved Max. The deep recesses of her mind had known it all along; the shock of his leaving her had brought it to the surface.

"Tired?" Jeffrey asked as he wheeled into the driveway.

"Very," she responded in a whisper. "I really want to get back to the apartment, Jeffrey. After I pick up my dog, I'd like you to take me on home. We can talk tomorrow." She longed to be within the privacy of her own tiny domain, so that she could give in to the tears she so stoically was holding in check.

"Well, you won't be taking McMutt home today. She had puppies last night, and Mom won't allow you to move the new mother and her six miniscule offspring. Mom is playing combination nurse and grandmother. She and McMutt have struck up a lasting relationship. It's very likely you've lost your dog for good. You know how Mom is about poor, homeless orphans."

"McMutt isn't an orphan," she protested. "She belongs to me."

Jeffrey came around the car to let her out. "But you have been gone so much lately. It's only natural that Mom should get attached to the lovable little mongrel. And vice versa."

It was true. Buffy saw immediately that she'd lost her dog to the capable Mrs. Dunstan, who had ensconced McMutt and her puppies in a comfortable wicker basket in the laundry room. Moving them to the apartment was out of the question.

The new mother lay on her side, giving nourishment to her newborn infants. Buffy leaned over her and patted her reddish-gold coat, which shone with health and careful attention.

The dog looked at her with large intelligent brown eyes, licked her hand, and lay her head back down contentedly. It was another good-bye, and Buffy's already broken heart further shattered into even tinier fragments. She stumbled out of the utility room, sobbing violently.

"Oh, dear." Mrs. Dunstan fussed around her. "Poor child. She's been through so much. Missing her wedding, stranded on that dreadfully primitive island for over a week. Do take her home, Son, she needs rest."

Jeffrey handled her with all the sensitivity of a good friend, instead of that of a lover. She knew she could never marry him and wondered how to break it gently, for she did care for this lanky blond young man, even if she couldn't love him.

"We'll talk tomorrow," he said gently as he stood in front of her apartment door. He seemed about to say something else but thought better of it as he uncomfortably watched her mop tears from her face with a trembling hand, which held a sodden mess of Kleenex.

Once alone in her apartment, she gave way completely and cried as she had never cried before in her life. There were practical matters of life she needed to attend to, such as unpacking, buying groceries, washing clothes; but all she could do was lie across her organdy bedspread, sobbing Max's name over and over.

If she'd just been more mature, if she'd just handled herself differently, perhaps she could have won him from Marlene. But all she had managed to do with her stupid antics was to send him right into Marlene's arms, which was probably where he was right this very minute. He was gone forever out of her life; she would never see him again. They hadn't even parted friends.

Around midnight she roused herself and got dressed for bed. Then she padded blindly into her bright, cheerful kitchen to fix herself a cup of coffee. Her cupboards were practically bare. There was only canned tomato juice and a box of stale Cornflakes settled in beside the jar of instant coffee. It didn't matter; she couldn't eat. Despite the fact that she hadn't had supper, the idea of food thoroughly revolted her.

After the coffee, she went to bed and wept some more, wondering how many rivers one must cry before a broken heart began to mend. She settled, finally, into a troubled, sad sleep.

Upon waking early the next morning, she discovered her face swollen like a balloon from her violent weeping. Cold water and makeup helped the swelling, but nothing could take away the shocked misery that deeply haunted lost amber eyes.

She was at the shopping center before the grocery store opened. After pulling her late-model car into a parking spot, she got out and wandered around, looking into shop windows and watching business people hustle their sleeping enterprises into the thriving commercial life of another new day. Bells on doors jangled as owners opened up and greeted her with a smile or a "good morning."

A little café was busily providing fast breakfasts to people on their way to work. She walked in. Sitting at the counter was a man with a wide muscular back and dark silky hair.

Her heart thumped wildly as she rushed over and touched him on the shoulder. A puzzled, strange face turned to her. Of course it wasn't Max.

"May I help you, miss?" asked a waitress from somewhere beside her.

"No—no," she stammered before fleeing out the door.

161

She squinted as a bright Miami sun prickled her eyes like a million needles. How crazy to think that just any man with a wide back and dark hair could be him. That man had worn a uniform bearing a Sunbeam bread emblem. He was a delivery man to the grocery store—a bread man who had stopped to get a cup of coffee before delivering his goods. A bread man!

She began to laugh hysterically. He probably had six kids, a house mortgaged to the hilt, and a nagging wife. She'd probably given him the thrill of the day by approaching him like that; he would think she'd been flirting.

She, along with a few other early birds, were the first ones into the grocery store. She strolled her cart around absently, looking at everything, seeing nothing. She passed other women who had come in with her, wondering if any one of them was suffering as she was. One couldn't tell by outward appearances, for she was behaving as calmly as they were. She didn't know what personal tragedies haunted their lives, and they couldn't tell what invisible agony she was experiencing.

After she had gotten halfway around the store, she realized her cart was still empty. She grabbed a box of laundry soap, threw it in, and tried to do a little mental meal planning. It was futile; her mind wouldn't function rationally.

She finally went to the deli and bought a couple of cartons of ready-made salads and a pound of sliced ham, forgetting entirely that she would need bread in order to fix sandwiches.

Mr. Dunstan came by late that morning to deal her another crushing blow. He'd hired someone to fill in for her while she was gone. She saw it as the beginning of the end of her job.

"I had to," he explained apologetically. "Our members were complaining about their youngsters not getting regular tennis lessons. Jeffrey met this new girl on the courts last week and seemed impressed with her." He cleared his throat uncomfortably and continued. "She's a Physical Education major at the University of Miami. Not as good

162

as you are, of course, but quite able to give regular tennis lessons. Her schedule fits in with ours perfectly, and, as I said, Jeffrey seemed quite impressed." He dropped off in embarrassment, and she sensed that Jeffrey had been more than a little impressed indeed. "Please understand that I'm not firing you," he assured her. "There's no reason why you and this new girl can't both give lessons. Of course, if you find a better job, I'll be glad to give you a good recommendation."

"That's very kind of you, Mr. Dunstan," she replied quietly.

"And I'd always be willing to help you any way financially. You know that."

"Of course." She smiled as he got up to leave. "I didn't get a chance yesterday to apologize to Mrs. Dunstan about not showing up for the wedding. I hope she is not angry. I know it must have been a lot of trouble for her to call everything off at the last minute."

"She was in a frenzy for a while," he admitted. "I'm afraid the wedding dress and a few other things she bought you have been sent back."

"I understand that. Were Jeffrey's relatives very disappointed about making the trip from Michigan for nothing?"

"Oh, no," he assured her. "They seemed very pleased to be taking a brief vacation in Florida. It's already freezing in Michigan this time of year. They used all our facilities here at the club and went away very happy."

"Well, I'm very glad that it turned out for the best."

He looked at her oddly before turning to go. "We are, too. Jeffrey will be coming by to see you later."

"Yes, he told me."

Mr. Dunstan harumphed and made a hasty exit, looking very glad to be doing so.

Jeffrey told her that afternoon that he felt they should postpone the wedding indefinitely. Several tournaments coming up was his excuse, but she knew it was because he too realized there was no real love between them and was trying to let her down gently.

She agreed without batting an eye, somehow feeling utterly abandoned as well as relieved. He had probably become interested in this new girl and was too kind to tell her. And she was too numb to tell him that it didn't matter—that she'd fallen irrevocably in love with a man named Max during the brief ten days she'd spent in paradise.

When he quizzed her about her short exile on what he presumed was a deserted island devoid of all modern luxuries, she sketched a broad, indefinite spectrum of facts, totally leaving out her shattering relationship with the man she had fallen in love with.

After he left, she got into her car and drove to the public beach. There were only a few brave bathers, for the weather had turned chilly and misty with unformed rain. Old retirees ambled the beach in search of treasures, finding only broken shells and an occasional empty soft drink can.

How different this was from Ponsonby's beach, with its sugar-white sand and blazing tropical sun. Memories rushed in and twisted her into knots of yearning. She haunted the drab, cold seascape, reliving every wonderful and poignant event that had taken place between herself and Max in that other world.

She left the beach and drove home in a blur of mental agony. Walking into the well-furnished, expensively carpeted lobby of her apartment building, she automatically went over to check her private mailbox. There was an advertisement and an envelope bearing the stamp of Palm Isle Resort.

Not being able to wait until she got to her apartment to open it, she halted in front of a plastic potted fern next to the elevator and tore into it with nervous fingers.

Disappointment swept over her in one huge, suffocating wave.

It was only her check for winning the tournament, signed by Maximilian Shepherd, Sr. With the check, which had a sizable figure that did nothing to lift her spirits, was a gracious letter also signed by Max's father, thanking her

164

for her participation in the tournament and congratulating her on her outstanding win.

When the elevator ascended abruptly, it didn't have the usual effect of plummeting the contents of her chest cavity into her stomach; grief had already done that.

It was so foolish to imagine that the envelope had contained a personal letter from Max. And when it didn't, even more ridiculous to think Mr. Shepherd would include with the check a chatty little note hoping her time spent on Ponsonby's Island with his son was enjoyable.

Max had probably filled him in on what a disaster it had been, and how he was finally glad to be rid of the troublesome little hooligan who had wrecked each separate day during his brief vacation away from the demands of his work by her crazy, thoughtless antics.

Her telephone was ringing when she entered her apartment. She threw her mail down on the desk before reaching to answer it.

"Hi, Buffy," came a familiar, high-pitched squeal over the line.

"Cindy! Gosh, it's good to hear your voice," Buffy answered weakly but with enthusiasm. And it *was* good to hear Cindy's youthful squeal. It was difficult to believe that it had been just over a week since she'd beaten her friend so soundly on the courts at Palm Isle. It could have been an eternity that had passed from then until now.

"Buffy, what's happening with you, anyway?" Cindy asked in concern. "I've been going absolutely bananas trying to figure out what's going on."

Cindy's voice came as if through a long tunnel. How inconvenient that her tennis buddies were scattered all over the United States, making it impossible to get together other than at tournaments. Cindy would be calling from her parents' home in Jersey. Buffy sat down in her desk chair, longing to talk to her friend face to face, instead of through miles of telephone cable.

"Well, I didn't marry Jeffrey."

"That is the only thing obvious to me," Cindy replied in a rush. "When I went up to Mr. Shepherd the night of the banquet, to tell him you wouldn't be there, he told me he was already aware of that. He said that you were with his son, that he had flown you out of Nassau, and that his plane had gone down on somebody's island."

"Lord Ponsonby's," Buffy put in.

"What?"

"It was Ponsonby's Island. He's a very wealthy Britisher who owns an entire island somewhere between here and the Bahamas. It was a beautiful place."

"Then you're okay?"

"Fine," she lied.

"When I told Mom your plane had gone down, she nearly went into hysterics," Cindy went on. "You know Mom. She was convinced all along that something dreadful would eventually happen to you. She accosted Mr. Shepherd after the banquet and urged him to call out the Coast Guard, the whole United States Navy, if necessary, to rescue you. He gave a kind of booming laugh and assured her in his best British accents that you were quite safe in the care of his capable son."

"That's right," Buffy replied. "I was."

"Well?" Cindy asked breathlessly. "What was he like?"

"Who?"

"The son, the son!" Cindy was growing impatient. "Tell me about him. Was he kind of cute?"

Kind of cute—that was like describing Albert Einstein as kind of smart. "Max was the most incredibly attractive man I've ever met in my life."

"Oooh," Cindy breathed. "Lucky you. I'll bet Jeffrey is jealous as all get out. By the way, have you two set a new date for the wedding?"

"No. I'll never marry Jeffrey."

"Oh, no," Cindy sympathized. "Is he awfully mad at you for being marooned on that island with Max? Oooh," she squealed, "I even like his name."

"I've only seen Jeffrey twice since I got back," Buffy explained to her friend. "He didn't seem angry at all. But we'll never get married to one another. I think that, if nothing else, is very clear."

166

But to Cindy it wasn't any clearer than mud. "But why? I don't understand."

"Because I don't love him and I'm sure he's not in love with me. I think both of us were blind when we got engaged; we just sort of drifted into it without really thinking." Buffy paused and there was a pregnant silence over the line. She knew her friend was seething with a whole battalion of unanswered questions. "Look," she said. "It's too hard to explain over the phone. This long-distance call must be costing your parents plenty."

"I'll pay for it myself," Cindy stated firmly. "Now tell me why you suddenly realized you're not in love with Jeffrey. You've always bragged about how compatible you two are."

She realized then what she'd known deep down all along: She and Jeffrey were not the least bit compatible. Compatibility had nothing to do with likes and dislikes; but was all tied up with desires and needs. "Let's just say that I saw the light." She laughed hollowly. "Jeffrey and I weren't meant for each other. I'm glad, at least, that I found out before it was too late."

Cindy's voice lowered from its high treble to a level slightly less shrill, which was meant to carry a threat. "Buffy, you're not leveling with me. Something really drastic has happened to you. I can read it in your voice. And it has to do with this man Max."

She was amazed at her friend's acumen. But then Cindy always did have a keen nose for scenting out the barest nuance of romance. She was a dreamy girl tied to overprotective parents and longing for the very thing her parents were so determined to shield her from.

"You're right," she admitted. "Something did happen to me—and it does involve Max."

"You're in love!" Cindy cried ecstatically. "It was love at first sight. Just like in the movies. You met him, looked into his eyes, and he into yours—and bingo!"

Her memory traced back to the first time she had gazed into his compelling gray eyes on the steps of his resort, and she trembled inside. "Yes," she agreed, finally admitting it to herself. "You're right. I never thought it happened like that, but I guess it does. I loved him right away, as if I'd known him since some time before the world was created."

"Oooh!" Cindy shuddered deliciously. "Has he proposed yet?"

She tried to give a laugh but choked on it. "No. It's all one way. Max was awfully nice to me, but he let me know in a million different ways that he considered me a child."

"But in the movies the guy always falls in love, too," Cindy argued, disappointed that things hadn't gone according to Hoyle. "The two people always get married and live happily ever after."

How was she to tell her young friend that real life wasn't anything like a Doris Day movie? She decided not to try—Cindy might have the unfortunate luck of finding this out for herself someday. Until such time, she would never understand how devastating it could be. She hoped that it would never happen to her friend, that she would go along in her rose-colored bubble for the rest of her life.

"There will be no 'happily ever after' for me, Cindy. Max and I parted on the worst of terms." She tried to inject a note of cheerfulness into her voice. "But don't you worry about me."

"No wonder you sound so funny. You're really hurt, aren't you? Listen, maybe if you got in contact with him and—"

"No," she cut in. "You don't understand at all. He is several cuts above me in every way. He's a man of the world, a titled aristocrat, a wealthy, fabulously attractive man. There's not one chance in a million that he would ever find someone like me appealing. Besides, he's involved with another woman."

"Oh, gosh!" Some of the hopelessness of Buffy's situation finally penetrated Cindy's veneer of youthful idealism. "I'm really sorry."

"Thanks."

"I guess there's nothing more to say."

"No. Look, I'll see you at the tourney in Syracuse next

month, maybe." Buffy felt the need to cry again and didn't want to break down over the phone. "Let's hang up. The bill must be close to ten dollars by now."

"Gee, I feel so sorry for you," Cindy commiserated.

"Well, I only knew him for a little over a week. It's impossible to have your life completely wrecked in that short period of time. I'll get over it," she assured her friend. But she knew she would never get over it. That ten days had been the bridge between ignorance and knowledge; childhood and the painful reality of adulthood.

"You take care now," she whispered in a soft southern voice. "I'll be okay." She managed to hang up before the flood came.

It turned cold that evening, and the sky opened up to weep. By now, however, she was pale and dry-eyed, her own tears spent. She was so dry, in fact, that she frequently licked her lips to moisten them.

Time passed in drab, tearless melancholy, and as her soul cried out for Max, her body did even more. All she could dream of was making love with him. Day and night she lived in a string of separate fantasies, each one ending the same way—ecstatic sexual fulfillment with him. It was unhealthy, this intense yearning after something she would never have. She began to wonder if she were losing her sanity.

Toward the end of the fourth day, she realized that she was pining away from her love for him. It was really ironic. She was the one who hadn't thought this kind of overpowering love possible. Max had told her it happened on occasion, and now he'd proven it.

She went for a long jog on the golf course. It was raining. She was the only one in a world of sloping greens and cool raindrops. She tried to grab for threads to pull her life back together. She couldn't go on like this. She still had herself, and the ability to play tennis within. She still had Wimbledon to look forward to—that was something.

But even this became an impossible dream as she opened her newspaper over a cup of coffee the next morning. Turning to the sports section first from force of habit, she saw bold headlines: TENNIS ACE SPENDS TEN DAYS IN ISLAND PARADISE WITH HOTEL MAGNATE.

Horrified, she crumpled the paper together accordion style, then forced herself to flatten it out to look again, hoping that her eyes had deceived her—as futile a hope as all her others. How had they gotten the story? Who could have given it to them?

Marlene. With sudden reeling conviction, she knew it had to have been her. Having Max had not been enough—Marlene wanted to spoil Buffy's career as well.

She read the article, discovering it contained nothing but facts. But how the facts had been loaded with innuendo! It was nothing that would constitute slander, yet full of hints and unanswered questions. It ended with: "And will fiancé Jeffrey Dunstan approve of Miss Vallentine's stolen bliss in this island hideaway?"

She saw her reputation running through her fingers like so much sand, and with it her hard-earned career. She'd been stripped of everything, and there was no one, no one to turn to.

The phone rang, and she moved through a haze of misery to answer it.

"Have you read the morning paper?" Jeffrey thundered at her.

"Y-yes. It's all lies."

"Who the hell cares. People will believe it. I almost believe it myself. You didn't tell me you were alone in a palatial house with the guy."

"Nothing happened."

"It doesn't matter. People will believe the worst. You've ruined me. How did they find out we were engaged?"

"Marlene Ponsonby, the daughter of the man who owns the island, must have let it out. Max is too honorable to do such a thing."

"Damn your eyes, Buffy, for getting me involved in this mess. You've made me look like a fool."

"Jeffrey, please, it's not my fault."

"I told you not to go off to that tournament in Nassau,"

he raved. "If you hadn't, none of this would be happening."

"And if I hadn't, we'd be married by now," she flashed back. "Have you considered that?"

"Yes, there's always a silver lining," he countered sarcastically. "I'm glad we didn't get married. Furthermore, we will *never* get married. And beyond that, I wouldn't come within ten feet of you now. The public will forgive the wronged fiancé, but never you. Stay away from me, Buffy," he warned. "You're poison."

She hung up on him quietly. So much for friends in time of need. She wondered if Max had seen the article. His plane would have been repaired, and he would be in Nassau by now, perhaps even on Caicos, building his new resort.

She toyed with the idea of calling him and rummaged around in her desk drawer for the brochure his father had sent her with the invitation to the tournament. She found it but chickened out when it came to actually picking up the receiver to ask the operator to connect her with the number of Palm Isle Resort.

No, she reasoned, Max wouldn't care about a little adverse publicity. Marlene had said he had the reputation for being a playboy, anyway.

CHAPTER 10

Buffy sat motionlessly over her cold coffee cup for several minutes, trying to envision her future. For the first time in her life, there was none. There was an absolute void—a complete nothing. Should she try to brazen this thing out? If she laid low for a while, perhaps in time people would forget, and she could make some sort of comeback.

But she could arrive at no answer; her mind was as muddled as her circumstances. It was death to be cut adrift like this with no one to turn to.

When the doorbell rang, she walked on leaden feet to open it. She saw Lord Ponsonby's flushed face before her and cried, "For heaven's sake, this is a surprise!"

His expression changed into a scowl as he said gruffly, "My dear child, you look quite ill. How I would like to get my hands around my daughter's throat for what she's done to you!"

"I'm all right. Come in." She impulsively pulled him through the door and motioned him to sit down. "It's wonderful to see you again. I never thought I would."

He sank into her couch with an exasperated huff. "I couldn't go back to my island without first coming to apologize to you. Max told me you worked at this country club, and a Mr. Dunstan I met at the pro shop was most informative about precisely where you were located."

"I'm so glad you dropped by. And please don't apologize for anything. Marlene obviously felt she was entitled to a little revenge. You're certainly not responsible for that. What can I fix you?" she asked hospitably, going over to open her refrigerator door.

Ponsonby peered around her tiny frame, which had become even tinier since he'd last seen her, and saw only a bottle of tomato juice and some deli cartons on the shelf in the refrigerator.

"How about a cup of coffee, or some tomato juice?" she asked, embarrassed that she couldn't offer a British lord anything more exotic. "I'm afraid I don't keep a bar in the apartment."

Ponsonby grinned enthusiastically. "Tomato juice, most certainly. The very thing."

She poured tomato juice into two of her best glasses, gave him his, then sat beside him on the couch.

"You haven't been eating," he accused.

"Of course I've been eating." She sipped her tomato juice with a show of enjoyment. "How is Loa?"

"She quit."

"Oh, no!"

"Yes. Had a deuce of a time getting her settled down into working for me again. She went berserk after you left, you know."

"Loa? Went berserk?" She couldn't picture gentle, sweet Loa doing such a thing.

"Absolutely bananas. She flew at Marlene like a mother hen defending her young. I finally pieced out of that garbled English of hers that she was dressing Marlene down quite thoroughly about how she had treated you and how she had made Max believe you were responsible for your and her spats, as it were. It was really quite fascinating to watch. Finally she stomped out of the house, saying she wouldn't stay on the same island with a woman like Marlene. Although I believe she used the descriptive term *snake* instead of woman. She stayed in her bungalow for two days, determined to fly out with Max when Myaka got his aeroplane mended. Myaka, of course, would have gone with her, and I would have been out two of the best servants a man ever had. I was in a regular quandry over the problem, as you can imagine. Meanwhile my palace went to shambles; Marlene wouldn't spoil her lily-white hands to do housework of any kind." He paused in his narrative and grinned at her impishly.

"What did you do?" she asked, infected, in spite of everything, by his ever-present good humor.

"Why, I got rid of Marlene!" It was a stunning admission, and Buffy's eyes flew open in astonishment. "Now I've shocked you." He placed his half-empty glass on the coffee table and eased back on the couch, making himself very much at home in her humble apartment. "I do love my daughter," he explained affably. "But where in the books does it say that I have to like her?"

"I naturally assumed—" she stammered.

"Being an orphan, you naturally assumed that all families got along like blackbirds in a pie. A common misconception, most likely, among your kind. Oh, yes," he replied to her uplifted brows, "Max told me you are an orphan. That's one reason I'm here today—to father you a bit. Lord knows I've never been able to do it for that conniving daughter of mine."

"B-but where did you send her?" She had a vision of him shipping Marlene off to a nunnery somewhere.

A satisfied smile curled his lips as he replied contentedly, "I sent her back to Madrid. There's a Spanish *conde* over there who wants to marry her. He's a stiff fellow, with a will of iron. Just the sort of husband my daughter needs. I told her if she didn't marry him, I'd cut off her allowance. That did it. She'd be lost without money. A woman like my daughter hasn't the wherewithal to earn it herself. She left for Madrid a while ago. That's why I'm in Miami—I brought her over yesterday so that she could make connections this morning. But apparently she couldn't leave without doing one last nasty piece of work on you. She must have called the paper from her hotel room yesterday afternoon."

"She sure did a job on me." Buffy shook her head and placed a petite foot on the coffee table as she leaned back into the couch dispiritedly.

"Ah, yes. Never have I seen the will to destroy so

clearly defined in a human being. It has been a great grief to me. She was absolutely enraged over the effect you were having on Max. Splendid man, Max." He turned toward her and eyed her speculatively.

"Mmm," she agreed dreamily. Then her eyes flew open in puzzled surprise. "What effect?" she demanded, turning toward him.

"Beg pardon?" He smiled mischievously.

"What effect was I having on Max? That *is* what you said, isn't it? That Marlene was angry about some effect I was having on Max?"

He shook his head and chuckled. "You really had no idea, did you? Such guileless innocence is most rare. But"—he wagged his finger at her reprovingly—"that dress you wore to the barbecue was not quite so innocent. If I were actually your father, I would have marched you back to your room to change."

She had the grace to blush, and Ponsonby threw his head back and laughed uproariously. "Oh, the look upon Max when you walked out in that thing. If ever a man was thoroughly besotted, it was he."

"Max, besotted? With me?" she asked in a high-pitched, disbelieving voice. "That's not true. He and Marlene are . . ." She waved her hand airily and declined to explain the situation to Ponsonby.

"Are what?" he pressed. ,

She was really uncomfortable now. She pressed her lips together tightly. Nothing could induce her to tell this nice man about the relationship Max had with his daughter. She wouldn't know how to begin even if she wanted to.

"Well?" he demanded.

"Let's change the subject," she suggested tightly.

"My dear child," he spoke incredulously, "from your reluctance to talk, I imagine you think there's something serious going on between Max Shepherd and my daughter."

Still trying to protect him, she remained silent.

"Who told you it?" He seemed to be having a difficult time deciding whether to laugh or to explode into anger.

"No need to answer that. It was Marlene who filled you with such rubbish."

"I heard it from her own lips," Buffy whispered softly.

"Dreadful liar, that child, always has been."

"Then they're not—I mean, they haven't—"

"Lord, no! Max has had a running contempt for Marlene since they were in rompers. He only tolerates her because he is a gentleman and is so fond of me. His attitude toward her has always been polite but distant. Even when he is somewhat friendly to her, she knows it's not genuine, which piques her no end."

"Then she doesn't love him, either?" These revelations were coming to Buffy so fast and furiously that she was having trouble assimilating them.

"She doesn't love anybody, my dear, but herself. And it hurts me deeply, because I can't account for it; I've given her everything. But that's another story entirely. Concerning the matter at hand, I can assure you in all honesty that she flirts with Max merely because he is a challenge."

"Are you absolutely sure about this, Lord Ponsonby?"

"Quite. Oh, long ago Lord Shepherd and I had hopes for their getting together. We even tried to throw them together once. Max was just out of prep school, and Marlene was home from her private school in England, too. We all went to Majorca on a lark. They both had a miserable time: Max because Marlene was there; Marlene because Max wasn't paying all her sophisticated and stunning looks any mind at all. He spent all his time on the tennis courts to avoid her. Lady Shepherd was alive then and was devastated. She hadn't seen her son for months, and here he was avoiding all social contact to keep away from Marlene. She raked both myself and Lord Shepherd over the coals thoroughly for arranging such a disastrous holiday. Oh, it was a miserable affair. Quite extraordinarily miserable." He shook his head and said with conviction that wouldn't allow the merest doubt, "No, if it's Marlene and Max having an affair that's been bothering you, set your mind at rest immediately. Such a thing is just not possible, now or ever."

177

"Oh!" she moaned, sickly realizing just how much she had wronged Max in accusing him. "Lord Ponsonby, what kind of reputation does Max have?" she asked fearfully.

"Do you mean, how are his morals?"

She nodded dumbly.

"Why, impeccable! Without blemish! If a man is irresponsible in his private life, he is usually considered irresponsible in business also. Max knows he can't afford that."

"Marlene told me he was sort of a . . ." She groped for a word. ". . . rake."

"Max! Heaven forbid. The man is a first-rate gentleman."

Of course he was! How could she have allowed Marlene to blind her to the obvious with her vicious lies? How could she have wronged him so?

"He's had women friends," Ponsonby went on to explain. "What single man his age hasn't? But there's been no hint of scandal of any kind. I understand he's considered quite a catch. But he has never shown the slightest inclination to get serious about anyone. This upsets Lord Shepherd frightfully. He had a marvelous relationship with Lady Shepherd and wants the same sort of happiness for his son. That's why I was so delighted when I saw how completely gaga he was over you."

"Well, if he was, he's not anymore," she sighed with great heaviness. "Not after the things I accused him of after I shoved Marlene into the pool. It must have been awful for him. And it's doubly unbearable for me to realize that I had a chance with him and blew it."

"You Americans and your odd expressions. Blew it, indeed." His crystal blue eyes danced. "If Max feels about you as I think he does, all you have to do is, reasonably, and with great deliberation, explain your stupidity and humbly ask his forgiveness. Now I know why he was like a man beside himself when he came back after bringing you to Miami. He hardly spoke to anybody. I tell you, one

178

would think he'd been shot right through with a kind of deadly nerve gas. But it will all come right."

"Do you really think I still have a chance with him?" she whispered, not daring to hope.

"Not a doubt in my mind, if you have the courage to try."

Buffy, who had never been short on courage, felt a small bubble of excitement begin to rise within her.

Lord Ponsonby, satisfied that the look of wounded misery had left her eyes, got up to go.

"Oh, thank you!" She gave him a brief, squeezy hug and kissed his round, full cheek.

"Save all that good stuff for Max," he chuckled. He left her a changed woman. He had carefully rebuilt what his daughter had torn down; for being a man of sadness, he insisted upon happy endings whenever possible.

She decided not to call Max, but to go straight to him in person. To see him again, to talk to him, was her goal. Beyond that, she would not plan. The happy momentum of moving toward some sort of destination quickened her body to new vigor. There was so much to do. At last she was busy.

She called the airport and booked a seat on the four o'clock flight to the Bahamas. That would give her a good six hours to get herself prepared to meet him again.

But what if he had already left for South Caicos? It didn't matter. If he was not in Nassau, she would get to South Caicos somehow. Swim there, if need be. To see him in flesh and blood again, and not just in dreams—the promise of it set her heart to singing.

She set her apartment to rights, tidying up and watering plants. It was something she'd been through a hundred times before leaving for tournaments. Then she went to the bank and cashed her tournament check.

With a purse full of money, she set off on an impulsive shopping spree. She would arrive in Nassau in style. She stopped in a cafeteria and ate an enormous lunch, the first real meal she had eaten in five days, then made a beeline for the beauty parlor.

"Do something with me," she said excitedly to the hairdresser as she wiggled herself into the smooth vinyl chair before a wall of mirrors.

The beautician thoughtfully regarded wildly disheveled honey curls, which framed a delicately boned face. "What do you have in mind?"

"Oh, I don't know. You're the expert. What do you think?"

The woman pulled out one tight curl and let it go. It sprang back against Buffy's head in exactly the same place it had been.

"We could straighten it," she mused.

"How long would that take?"

"About two hours."

"I can't afford the time."

"I wouldn't recommend it, anyway. Curls are in style. You're fortunate to have them naturally. Your hairdo, as it is, suits your facial structure. Let's just wash it, trim it, and not mess up a good thing."

Buffy came out of the beauty shop with her hair looking much the same as it did when she had gone in, except it was even fluffier and more piquantly feminine. Unknowingly, she had found the one beautician, perhaps, in a million, who didn't insist upon ruining a person.

Next she went to the Petite Shop and combed the dress racks. She bought two dresses, but as the cashier was ringing them up she noticed a mannequin dressed in a straight, floor-length garment the color of fresh cream, elegant in its simplicity. It's only adornment was a soft ruffled yoke. The dress could be worn to a formal dinner party or to a casino—it was that versatile. It would even make a lovely wedding gown.

"I want that," she said impulsively.

"That's the last one," the saleslady spoke ruefully. "It has been a popular item, and we only ordered one in each size. It's rather exclusive and quite expensive."

Buffy looked at the tag and discovered that indeed it was not cheap. When she also saw that the dress was a size five, she insisted. "It's my size. I'll buy it."

The saleslady looked dubious, as if she didn't want to go to the trouble of stripping the mannequin. "Perhaps I could interest you in something else," she said. "We have some lovely formal dresses over by the wall."

Buffy's temper began to simmer. "I want that dress. Now, are you going to get it for me, or do I have to speak to the manager of this store?"

The woman, realizing she was dealing with a stubborn girl, relented with a sigh and attacked the dummy.

Buffy left the store with her parcels, making a beeline for a shop that specialized in lingerie, where she happily went mad buying scraps of lace, chiffon, and ribbon. All for Max, not at all certain that he would ever see them but willing to gamble, all or nothing, that he would. She topped everything off by splurging on a long satin robe of blushing rose.

Once back in her apartment, she began the feverish but methodical process of packing. Only three hours until blast-off. With her luggage lying on the bed, still open and packed to the hilt with neatly folded clothes, she padded off to take a luxurious, perfumed bath.

Then she wriggled into new underthings, choosing the most transparent of the lot. Thus attired, she sat down and put on her makeup, taking great pains to create a flawless, bright-eyed look.

Two hours left: she was ahead of schedule. As she reached for a slip and the new slate-blue dress she'd laid out to wear, the doorbell rang.

She uttered a crisp curse and decided to ignore it. It was probably that little boy down the hall selling magazine subscriptions again. It sounded like his demanding, insistent ring. She stood still, slip in one hand, dress in the other, waiting for him to go away.

But he didn't. He just rang and rang, apparently becoming so impatient that he leaned against the bell with the intentions of going on in this fashion, if need be, forever.

She slapped the clothes on the bed in a fit of pique, grabbed for the rose-colored robe, which lay neatly folded in one of the suitcases, swiftly buttoned herself into it, and

181

marched to the door irritably, intending to give the little beggar a piece of her mind.

When she opened the door, she was startled beyond sensibility. Max stood before her, wickedly handsome in an oyster-colored business suit, a crumpled edition of the *Miami Times* clutched in one angry fist. To say that he was enraged would have been an understatement.

"Have you seen this!" He shook the tattered paper at her, then brushed past her into the apartment. "I'm so damn beside myself, I could bite nails."

This wasn't at all as she had envisioned their reunion would be. There were no bright lights of passion, no locked embraces, no singing angels. Perhaps Ponsonby had been wrong about how Max felt about her. After all, could a man who kept a crocodile around to scare guests be completely relied upon? Flames of doubt licked at her confidence and threatened to consume it.

He threw the paper on the coffee table and growled savagely, "That Marlene! What I would do if I could get my hands on her!"

"She's horrible," Buffy agreed. "I know too that she told me awful lies about you. But I suppose you wouldn't be interested in hearing how sorry I am that I believed them."

"Not in the least," he rapped out curtly. "Right now I'm more concerned about the problem at hand."

So much for Ponsonby's theory of wooing Max with soft apologies. Her shoulders slumped despairingly.

He paced the room like a restless panther. "Do you have any idea what this kind of rumor could do to my reputation if I don't put a stop to it? Already the staff at Palm Isle are looking at me as if I'm some kind of maniac who specializes in corrupting little girls."

"Well, it hasn't been a parade of lights for me lately, either," she countered. "I've lost everything—my job, my career, even my dog. Jeffrey and his family won't come near me, not that I give a tinker's damn."

He pivoted on his heels. "Then you're not marrying Dunstan?"

She laughed hollowly. "It's off for good."

"That's the best news I've heard all day." He scoured the apartment with determined gray eyes, which finally lighted upon her telephone. Within moments he'd gotten through to his father in Nassau.

"Dad? It's all set. The wedding is on. Go ahead with the plans. Remember, keep it small but elegant, romantic yet dignified. Plenty of flowers. Invite only one reporter. We must convince him that this is a love match of the highest order. That should nip in the bud any further scandalous speculation concerning my relationship with Buffy." He paused, then answered, "Oh, yes, she's agreed."

She didn't know whether to feel ecstatic or outraged.

He whipped out his arm and consulted an expensive gold wristwatch. "Yes, seven o'clock. I'll pack her up, and we'll be there in plenty of time."

Pack up, indeed! Just like a basket of ripe Florida fruit. Pack it up—ship it out, all nice and tidy.

"Get the staff busy preparing the bridal suite for us. You know, champagne, pheasant under glass, the whole bit. It will give their tongues something better to wag about than my imputed state of debauchery. What? All right, filet mignon. You get the picture. Right. Bye, Dad."

He hung up and shot Buffy a steady look that brooked no nonsense. She glared at him frostily.

"You will marry me tonight," he ordered.

"I heard."

He turned toward the window that led onto her small balcony and, flinging his suit jacket back, stuffed his hands in his pockets. "We'll take off for England tomorrow, for a month of honeymooning. By the time we get back the scandal will have been forgotten about. We'll come back here, settle up loose ends, and then you will come and live with me on my yacht at Caicos while I build my resort. I've already ordered that the tennis courts be poured first, so that I can continue to coach you."

"How considerate of you."

"Don't get sarcastic with me, Buffy. You need me, and you know it. When the time comes, I'll take you to Wimbledon. You'll win, and your fondest dreams will come true."

She remained silent. What did he know of her fondest dreams? "What of love?" she finally asked softly, moving over to grasp the back of a chair for support. "You were the one who insisted that a marriage shouldn't take place without it."

He drew a deep, ragged breath, all his agitation being replaced by a private agony. Slowly he walked to the couch and sat down, bending his dark silky head in his hands in utter dejection.

"I have enough for both of us," he spoke lowly. "I've loved you since I saw you play in Lauderdale last spring. It was I who asked Dad to organize the tournament at Palm Isle and invite you."

This turnabout had the effect of nearly cutting her legs out from under her. She opened her mouth in mute astonishment.

"Everything I've done has been an effort to express my love for you. Every movement I made, every word I spoke while we were on Ponsonby's Island was a subtle declaration of love. I thought I was making headway before Marlene showed up. You know, you killed me when you believed those lies. I was angry enough to deliver you into my rival's arms, but lord knows what it cost me to do it. I felt like a dead man when I left that airport."

Max was falling apart before her eyes. It was like watching the Rock of Gibraltar crumble into the sea. All because he was in love with her. She didn't know what to say.

He leaned forward and clasped his hands before him. They trembled. "These past days have been hideous. I can't live without you. I had already made up my mind to come back and try to win you from Dunstan, putting off the building of Caicos for weeks, if necessary." The loving gray eyes he turned upon her had the effect of melting every already paralyzed bone in her body. "I've looked for you all my life, Buffy, but I realize that you've only known me two weeks, that you're not ready for love, that

184

you are young." Leaning back on the couch, he looked up at the ceiling and swallowed thickly. "I'm prepared to woo you after we marry, to bring you around to loving me."

"That won't be necessary," she whispered in a voice barely audible.

"Please."

This was Max begging; it was incredible. "No. I mean . . ." Oh, couldn't she say anything right? She gave up trying to explain her love in words and turned to physical action, her old standby.

Rose satin whispered to the floor, and she climbed agilely into his lap before he knew what was happening, tiny bits of see-through lace brushing tantalizing across his well-tailored suit.

She knew what to do, for she had spent many hours dreaming of nothing else. She kissed his mouth and twined her fingers in his soft dark hair. A passion was released within her that set her body on fire.

"I love you," she pledged against his lips, and said it over and over again as she kissed the hollows of his face, beautiful silver eyes now closed, clean masculine mouth, which opened to drink thirstily.

"Oh, god," he moaned. "I've been half crazy from need of you." He massaged golden skin, satin white skin, and pulled at little bits of lace covering places he wanted to touch.

"I was coming to you." All coherent thought began to softly flee away. "I'm ready. My wedding dress, everything. I'm ready, you'll see. . . ." An exquisite ecstasy overpowered all contact with reality.

He eased her down on the couch and feasted on her body. And she writhed to meet every kiss. She held her hands around his head as it traveled downward to claim every inch of her warm, intimate womanliness, finally kissing where he gave her such an intense, pleasurable desire for fulfillment that she shuddered and cried out from the urgency of it.

He lifted his head and buried it in her midsection, panting heavily, groping for control. "Shh! Be still," he ordered on a ragged indrawn breath.

"Please. Oh, please, Max," she sobbed.

"I will. Tonight."

And he did. In the honeymoon suite of Palm Isle Resort. Twice before midnight. Both times very properly.

But that was Max Shepherd—always the proper gentleman.